Walking the Invisible Line

A Line That Barely Exists

By

Alton R. House

ISBN
978-1-956529-06-7 (Paperback)
978-1-956529-05-0 (eBook)

Table of Contents

A Gangster's story of nine individuals. Has set forth goals of control and conquer. Not like any other Gangster's you might have heard about before. These individuals are tactical, and military trained. Very bright & intelligent, but with a dark twisted outlook on society, and economy. Paul a very high classed Realtor that has more going on than just buildings going up. He pulls together connections that he remembers from the military. With special forces, and tactical training. This group is more than just a mob; they are a force to be reckon with! Now if you thought Nino Brown from New Jack City; Beans from State Property; and Tony Montana from Scarface was something. Ha! Meer Amateurs! Now for you Gangster lovers here's something for you!

{The Meadows Crew}
Paul aka Meadows
Richard Miles aka Right Hand
Lavis Coltrane aka Links
George Matthews aka Gatz
Brandon Wiley aka Butcher
Kym Lei aka Digits
Samantha Hues aka Siren
Rachel Gaines aka PG1
Porshia Brown aka PG2

CHAPTER 1

THE REUNION

PAUL CONTACTS RICHARD

{Paul} Now is the time to get things in order. I've been working on how to take this to a whole new level. I'm going to give my good friend Richard a call, and then we can get the old platoon back together again.

{Paul Calls Richard}

{Richard} Hey honey! Can you get that for me?

{Richard's Wife Answers the Phone}

{Patricia} Hello!?!

{Paul} Why hello Patricia, and how are you? This is Paul. How are you guys been doing?

{Patricia} Hi Paul, and how you're doing!?! We've been doing fine Paul! Oh my Gosh! It's been such a long time since we heard from you! I guess you want to speak with Richard.

{Paul} Yes! I certainly would love to speak to Richard. If it's not any trouble?

{Patricia} Trouble! No trouble at all Paul, hold on! Richard! Richard Honey!

{Richard} Yes Babe! What is it?

{Patricia} Pick up! Phone for you.

{Richard} Hello?

{Paul} Well hello Richard haven't heard from you in a long time.

{Richard} Well! Well! Well! I didn't expect to hear from my old military buddy! Damn it's been a long time!

{Paul} Yes it has Richard! Look, I need to meet with you ASAP!

{Richard} Sure, but what's it all about?

{Paul} I have a Serious Business Proposition for you, but nothing discussed over the phone.

{Richard} Hey well, you surely got my curiosity going.

{Paul} Don't worry! We'll talk about it later when we meet up.

{Richard} Damn! Secret Service Style Again!?!

{Paul} Yes Sir! Secret like that, and then some.

{Richard} Well then Paul, I'll meet you at 1900 hrs. at the Mexican restaurant downtown. You know the place.

{Paul} Good! I'll see you then.

{At 1900 hrs. Richard Meets Paul at The Restaurant}

{Richard} Hey Paul! What's good with you Bro!?!

{Paul} Hey Richard my man! Damn It's been a long time!

{Richard} True indeed! True indeed! So, what is this Serious proposition of yours. That you can tell me over the phone?

{Paul} Well first off! Do you still have the numbers from our old crew?

{Richard} What!?! Back from the military?

{Paul} Yes! The Other Seven Members from our squadron.

{Richard} Yes, I believe so. I know three of the numbers, but the others I know where they work at.

{Paul} Cool! I need you to get in contact with them ASAP!

{Richard} Man! Are you going to tell me? What's this All About!?!

{Paul} Okay, through the years I have gotten a lot of connections. Some through the crew, but most on my own. In which to be able to run a Major Operation. Man, I'm talking about Control and Conquering!

{Richard} What!?! The Drugs and Gun Cartel?

{Paul} Yes! You got it Rich! Everything across the board, and corner the market.

{Richard} Man! Are you crazy, or what!?!

{Paul} Hell no I'm not! As a matter of fact; I'm fully aware, and in my right mind!

{Richard} Yeah that just went left!

{Paul} You don't understand. We can run this nation. Not just the region, or state.

Besides; you don't really want to do you dirt close to home anyway!

{Richard} My GOD Paul! Are you aware of what you're saying? Besides! I don't think our old people could handle such a task that big!

{Paul} Trust me Richard. It will work to our advantage. I got connections all over. Even across seas. I'm talking about Columbia; Hawaii; Philippians; just to name a few. I also got cops in the pocket, Judges on speed dial; two of the top lawyers money can buy! They're a husband and wife team. Have you heard of The Manning Law Firm!?!

{Richard} I sure have! You got them on your team!?!

{Paul} Damn Skippy!

{Richard} Wow! You got all this on lock, but you still need a massive crew to pull this off.

{Paul} Richard. You are my right hand! You're the only one I can trust to help me accomplish this task. You are the one who will report to me and relate to the crew of what to do. Once you confirm contact with everyone let me know so we can move forward. Don't worry things will not interfering with your 9 to 5's. In fact, don't the old crew have great jobs?

{Richard} Yes, they do.

{Paul} Good! I don't need no B.A.F in my organization!

{Richard} BAF's!?!

{Paul} Broke Ass Folks! Get my drift?

{Richard} Damn! Got it! Well I'm going home for now, but I'll get on this first thing tomorrow morning.

{Paul} Great! And the sooner; the better!

{Richard} My first contact out the gate, is Lavis.

{Paul} Most definitely, and don't forget George; Brandon, and let's not forget the ladies!

{Richard} Oh No! Let's not forget them. Besides! They're crazier than we are! You know damn well we need them.

{Paul} Well goodnight Richard!

{Richard} Goodnight Paul! Time for me to get home before the little lady starts to miss me!

{As Paul and Richard Goes Their Separate Ways for The Evening. Paul Receive a Call from One of His Connections}

Richard contacts Lavis

{Richard Calls Lavis}

{lavis} Hello.

{Richard} Hello Lavis It's been a long time my brother. No see or hear from.

{lavis} Who is this!?!

{Richard} Lavis! It's Richard! You don't remember your old buddy from the military!?!

{lavis} Richard? My GOD! It's been a long time since I heard from you!

{Richard} Yep the and only.

{lavis} Man Damn! Now it's getting ready to snow; in the middle of July! Cause I haven't heard from you since our platoon left the war in Afghanistan.

{Richard} Well I'm still kicking it strong, and still alive!

{lavis} Oh that's suppose too be a good thing!?!

{Richard} Oh that's cold! Well look my man; the reason I'm contacting you is that our friend; Paul needs us to pull our old squadron back together again. But this time it's for a whole different reason.

{lavis} I can only imagine, so what Paul got in mind for the squad to get together again?

{Richard} Control and Conquer!

{lavis} Control what!?! Drugs; Guns, supply what's in demand!?!

{Richard} Yep! Any, and everything he can supply and demand.

{lavis} Say what!?! How he expects to pull that off?

{Richard} Well he's got the connections. Local, and international. Plus, you still got the connections you had since the war?

{lavis} Yeah, I do!

{Richard} Good! We can utilize those links to be on top of our game.

{lavis} Well look, we got to contact the ladies, also George and Brandon.

{Richard} So are you in, or out?

{lavis} Yep count me in!

{Richard} Yes, my brother! Ok. Now you got to call George, and Brandon. I'll call, and deal with ladies.

{lavis} Now Rachel and Porshia may be easy, but Kym on the other hand. Might be harder to convince.

{Richard} Don't worry, I know how to work with Kym!

{lavis} Ok Richard, I'll see you later. We got moves to make, and time is of the essence.

{Richard} You got good buddy! See you later!

{Richard and Lavis departs ways from one another. To get the crew together again. The next day, lavis contacts Richard for any new progress}

{lavis} Hey Rich! What's going on man!?!

{Richard} Nothing much Lavis, so what's going on your end?

{lavis} Well I got in contact with Brandon, and he said, He will link up with George this evening when he gets off from work, so did you get in contact with any of the ladies?

{Richard} Yes, I did! Kym was the first one! She said, "She's going to get the girls together. It looks like everything is coming into place.

{lavis} It certainly looks that way, and when are we all going to meet with Paul!?!

{Richard} Saturday at that old warehouse. On Lexington and 3rd.

{lavis} Ok I know the spot. Right on the corner.

{Richard} Yep! That's the one. At 1600 hrs. soldier!

{lavis} Yes Sir! 1600 hrs. Sir! Ha! Ha! Cool man! See you then!

{Paul calls Richard to see if he made any accomplishments for The Control, and Conquer Move}

{Richard} Everyone is in place, and ready to go! I told them the time; place; and all. It's all set Paul!

{Paul} Good! Everything is going according the plan. Nothing can stop it now!

{Richard} Hell not even the police, shucks you got them on lock too! Paul, you're a bad man!

{Paul} You better believe it Rich! A Bad Man!

THE GATHERING

{Paul} Well Richard, where is everybody? Now you know how I am about being on time.

{Richard} Don't worry, lavis said that, they would be here. Look their here now.

{lavis} What's up Rich? Ha! Look at here! Look at here! Paul Meadows.

{Paul} lavis, how are you? Look at here. George; Brandon; Rachel; Porshia; Samantha and the remarkable Ms. Kym.

{Kym} Hello Paul. George; Brandon; Richard. lavis like I said I'll have the girls together with me. You know how we do!

{Richard} Well Paul we're all here! Now enlighten us on this plan of yours.

{Paul} Ladies and Gentlemen. Have a seat. Now, what I'm a tell you guys it's strictly confidential. It goes no further than this room. For the past five years, I've been working on some angles. Connections and investments. To the point where I have links across seas. With my crew by my side, we will own and corner the market. No one can be able to stop us! No way! No How!

{George} Paul, why are you trying to take on the Roll of Scarface!?! Be who you are, and not like some mobster.

{Paul} Look guys! All I'm saying is, The Meadows Crew would be the new invisible mob. Not like no ordinary mob. More like an invisible line!

{Richard} Yes! We will be better than a mob! We would roam like thieves in the night. Stick and move! Not being all out in the open with a bunch of drugs and guns. Acting like it's all about us.

{Kym} Correct! We got to move like a stealth.

{Paul} I can tell you guys like this, we're walking the invisible line! A line that barely exists. And what that means is, everything is incognito mode. Nothing out and abroad.

{Samantha} Now Paul, true we've been through thick and thin together as a platoon but being as a new mob family!?! Humph! I don't know about that.

{Paul} I can assure you Sam, that nothing will go wrong. Unless we allow it.

{Rachel} No matter what you do in life, things can go wrong in a blink of an eye.

{Paul} As a matter of fact, I have some important investments to make. I'm getting in contact with a point man.

{lavis} What do we need with a point man for!?!

{Paul} To make sure our product reaches its destination. Clean, and or otherwise.

{Kym} Alright Paul, what do you have on the inventory list that your marketing?{George} Ha-Ha! I hear you talking, but how are we going to take over like that? Furthermore, how many crews are out here!?!

{Lavis} So true George. Too much competition out here.

{Paul} Look you guys, we are not going to be one of those so-called dealers. wannabe gangsters! Nothing, but pranksters! We are a true family, and family always stick together.

{Samantha} Yes Paul, we have Special Tactical Training, but that's military! We'll have to wipe out majority of them street hoods!

{Paul} No we don't, and I don't plan on that kind of tactic. What I'm talking about is. Nobody will supply these crews. Drug lords, and even gun runners! The Meadows Crew will be the only ones who will supply them all!

{Kym} Damn! You got it on lock like that Paul!?!

{Paul} Yes ma'am, and then some!

{Brandon} Now let me get this straight! You got the connections in place. Ok now I hate to even ask, but what if we get crossed by anyone?

{Paul} Oh yeah, Violators will pay the ultimate price! They will Disappear!

{Rachel} I'm guessing that we all hold our same positions from the war, but on a different level huh!?!

{Paul} You got it Rachel. We're the major suppliers! And all these wannabe dealers. Are our customers, or shall I say; consumers! Ok Richard you already know your position.

{Richard} Roger Paul!

{Paul} Lavis, you're Links. George, you still got the gun connections on lock?

{George} Yes, I still have the guns on lock. I never lost my touch, nor connects for fire power.

{Paul} Good! We need plenty for street sales. Brandon aka Butcher, and you still running your meat markets?

{Brandon} Paul, I have three meat markets. With five major distributors across the nation; and including Mexico.

{Paul} Excellent! It will come in handy I can assure you. Now Rachel and Porshia. You two are my PG's 1&2. My Point Guards. You two will assist with the guns, and the ones who crosses us! Anyone who talks, or tells anything about our meet discussion, and you too can disappear without a trace! Is that understood Meadows Crew!?!

{Everyone answers simultaneously} Yes Sir!!

{Paul} Alright, and always remember. True Gangster's, rolls in silence! And like no other! You tell anything on social media. Fake Ass Gangster's boast on everything they do! That's why, and how they get caught up. We don't do that. We just make shit happen and move forward. We don't war, unless we have too. Let the local gangs do that. True Gangster's don't dwell in the hood all day. We get money, because we have money working for us. All around the board! The core of it all is that; We're walking an invisible line! A line that barely exist. Now! Are there any questions?

{Richard} No questions, just conclusions. We have shipments coming in next week. The first shipment is roughly a total of $60 million. Containing School Supplies; Fabrics; Guns and Ammo; and of course, Drugs!

{George} Damn Paul, what in the world you got going on here?

{Lavis} Seems like a lot. That Paul got going on! No holding back.

{Kym} Now where are you planning on distributing the products at?

{Paul} Well first off, I have several warehouses along the East Coast. From New York to Florida! Also, building up shops in Texas; Michigan; and subsequently California. This is just to name a few of the states that I have right now. So, you see, I really need you guys. This a Multi-Billion Dollar business.

{Samantha} Wow! That's a lot of territories to cover, are you sure about this Paul?

{Paul} I'm more than sure, I can personally guarantee it!

{Kym} Damn Paul! Now I see how you get down. True genius at work. Now we're doing this like we did in Afghanistan, code verb! See something but say nothing!

{Paul} Exactly Kym!

{Lavis} Now what about our businesses?

{Paul} You all get to keep your businesses going as usual! Just know that; I will be in contact with you guys very soon. You don't have to change a damn thing! Because everything will come into play. Well that's it for now, class dismissed.

{As everyone's leaving the office. Paul speaks with Richard.}

{Richard} Paul, I really hope you got everything figured out!?!

{Paul} Richard! I'm really counting on you man. Now I trust my crew, but I'm depending on you. So, you got my back right!?!

{Richard} Most definitely my brother, I got you!

{Paul} I knew I can count on you Rich! Rest assured no one else could be able to help me pull this off like you.

{Richard} Well Paul, we got a lot to do, so we better get cracking at it!

Paul Ties Up Loose Ends

{Paul} Ok, I'm going to get in contact with Montego.

{Richard} Who's Montego!?!

{Paul} He's one of my contacts, in which he has connections in different area codes; merchandise and shipments. He helps me to eliminate the middle man.

{Richard} Yes! A major savings in the trade game.

{Paul} Exactly right Richard! You connect with the crew, and I'll talk with Montego.

{Paul reaches out to Montego}

{Paul} Alright Montego! I got things in operation! All Hands-on Deck! My people are ready. I got the documents that needs to be signed.

{Montego} Don't worry Paul, everything is in place at the office. Kym has the documents filed. Now remember, next Saturday the shipment is coming from Venezuela.

{Paul} Good! That's 60 million coming in.

{The phone rings for Paul, and it's Richard}

{Paul} Hey hang on for a second Montego. Richard, what happen to you? I was calling you all morning!

{Richard} Look at here, I've been taking care of some loose ends. That needed to be adjusted. We can't afford anything going wrong. Everything got to be tight and right!

{Paul} Very well, have you spoke to George? Because next week our shipment will be coming in. And I'm talking about 60 million worth of supplies.

{Richard} So the crates of steel must be in there also Huh!?!

{Paul Yes, plus crates of that fine china, and enough snow to freeze New York City! On top of that, each one of our "Meadows" has employees working under them.

{Richard} Ok, I'm going to call George, and Lavis so we can discuss the details about next weekend.

{Paul} Alright, don't forget what we talked about telling everybody everything!

{Richard} Don't worry Paul, I got it under control.

CHAPTER
2

MAKING MOVES

{George} Hey Lavis, check this out. Richard just called me to let us know. That next weekend the shipment is coming in, so we got to be ready to make this move.

{Lavis} No sweat George! Everything is in order, so how big is the shipment?

{George} How does $60 Mill worth sounds to you!?!

{Lavis} Got Damn! That's huge!

{George} Exactly! Now when I say, everything is going to be in the shipment, I mean everything!

{Lavis} Ok then, I'll have the trucks ready to go. All I need to know is the time. So that they'll be in place.

{George} Good deal! As soon as Rich get back in contact with me about the day and time, I'll let you know.

{Lavis} Sounds good, are you going to get in contact with Brandon? To let him know what's going on for next weekend.

{George} Most definitely, Rich is going to let Kym know so she can get with the girls.

{Lavis} Good, you know George; one thing about this crew. We can make things happen at the drop of a dime.

{George} Damn straight!

{Lavis} We are in a new day and time. Nothing can stop us now!

{George} Alright, now I'm about to call Brandon, and then Richard. To see what time next weekend.

{Lavis} Good to go! No time for games.

{George} Alright let's get it together!

{Now George is contacting Brandon about the meet next weekend}

{George} Hey what's going on Brandon?

{Brandon} Hey George, nothing much. I'm at my market in Nashville. What's up?

{George} I was wondering if you know about next weekend?

{Brandon} Yep! The big shipment, on Saturday at 5pm.

{George} Well Damn! I'm glad to know that you're up on the news.

{Brandon} Yeah, Paul filled me in. Being as which, he's going to call me back around 4 this afternoon.

{George} Oh ok, so now it's all on the ladies to be informed.

Meeting in The Ladies Room

{Kym} Ok Ladies, things are in full swing. The fellas got their stuff together, and we got to tighten up our end.

{Samantha} Ok, so for me in concern I still hold my position as siren!?!

{Kym} Yes! You let us know when local authorities are moving in. Just like from the war. You have the influence, and the intelligence to get certain information. To stay ahead of the game!

{Samantha} Oh no doubt! I can do that, also I have the stuff. To make people talk.

{Kym} You mean!?!

{Samantha} Uh huh! The Truth Serum! Hell 1ml. of that stuff, and you'll be singing like a canary!

{Kym} Wow! Just like the good old days! When we want them to talk, dammit they talk!

{Samantha} You got that right girlfriend! I like to call it Triple S. The Serious Snitch Serum.

{Kym} Hell yeah! Perfect name for it. Now Rachel and Porshia, PG's 1 and 2. You ladies will assist George with the weapons, also if anyone gets out of line, you'll already know what to do!

{Rachel} Affirmative!

{Porshia} No problem! Consider that a done deal.

{Kym} Now George will contact you ladies about next weekend. That a major shipment is coming our way. Lavis said that he got trucks ready to go, and we'll need to be just as ready to roll out as well.

{Samantha} Don't worry Kym! We got it under control. Besides Brandon got to get back in contact with me, and you know how he do with the blades. Especially when it comes to meat! And I'm not talking about hamburger, or steak neither.

{All the ladies say simultaneously} Yeah, we know! Chop! Chop! Slice! Slice! Uh oh
Minced Meat!}

{Porshia} Hell yeah! Brandon can throw a blade at 5ft. and hit someone right dead in the head!

{Kym} Damn straight!

{Rachel} Ok, so next Saturday we can be expecting the shipment.

{Kym} I would say that's a safe bet. Even though anything can happen.

THE DAY BEFORE
THE SHIPMEN

{Rachel} Now Kym, what about our workers? If anyone hears about what we got going on, it's a rap!

{Samantha} Don't worry about that! and if anybody does hear anything, they better not say anything to anybody, or they're going to disappear!

{It's now the day before, and Paul is making sure things are tight and right.}

{Paul} Alright Lavis, did you get in contact with the truckers?

{Lavis} Yeah, I spoke with them yesterday, and everything is set to go. We have eight trucks that's suitable for the haul.

{Paul} Perfect! We have everything we need for the weekend.

{Lavis} Now the crew needs to be on time. So what time do we start loading up?

{Paul} Saturday at 6pm. This way the area will be shut down, but I have a connection working on the inside. So that we can work through the night.

{Lavis} I see we can work all night until the break of day. I'm going to call Brandon, and Kym. They can get everyone else together.

{Lavis calls Brandon}

{Brandon} Hey Lavis, where are we supposed to meet at on Saturday?

{Lavis} Ok, Paul has given me the details for where we meet. We'll meet at the Pearson's Dock at 6pm.

{Brandon} Yeah; we all know the place, but is Paul serious about this? $60 million worth of product and supplies.

{Lavis} Yes, he is very serious about this! And we'll be heavily armed too! Strapped to the tee, and our soldiers humph, they don't play!

{Brandon} Well I hope Paul tied all the loose ends. Cause there's no room for errors!

{Paul} So what is Brandon going to do?

{Lavis} He'll be there, and won't you be there also?

{Brandon} I certainly will.

{Lavis} Alright Brandon, see you guys tomorrow. Now don't forget to call Richard and Kym.

{Paul} Don't worry about Richard! Cause he already knows.

{Kym} Hello Lavis. Everybody is ready for the shipment tomorrow.

{Lavis} Yep! All systems go for tomorrow, at the Pearson's Dock 6pm.

{Kym} Sounds good! I'll tell the ladies the time. In fact, I'll bring them with me.

THE BIG DAY

{Paul} Well, well! Look at here; look at here! The time has come, to put our plan in operation. Alright fellas, let's get these trucks loaded! Hell; we got a lot to load between now, and 3'o clock in the morning.

{Richard} Why!?! What's going down at 3 in the morning?

{Paul} Because that's when these trucks roll out of here. All eight has their designated areas to go to.

{Lavis} That's right! When these trucks are filled, they'll be ready to move out. Each one has the same amount of stock for each destination.

{Richard} Great! So, when they arrive at the appointed destination. Do you have anyone specifically for each shipment?

{Paul} Why yes as a matter of fact, each one of you shall go with a truck. To make sure each shipment makes it there.

{Lavis} Paul! Now why you didn't tell us this at the meeting? Now we got to rearrange everything!

{Paul} Not necessarily, you see; I got everything under control. Unless you guys forgot, it's Saturday evening.

{Lavis} So!

{Paul} So nothing, tomorrow is Sunday! Hell, where do you guys work at on a Sunday? No damn where!

{Kym} True, Not false!

{Samantha} He got you there Lavis.

{Brandon} Well you guys are going to stand around talking, or are we going to get these trucks loaded, so we can get out of here.

{George} I sure hope so. Enough talking about it, time to be about!

{Rachel} Alright crew let's get it!

{Richard} Wow it is now 2am in the morning. I got to call my wife and let her know that I must travel out of town. To handle some business.

{Paul} Well do what you got to do!

MOVING ON

{Paul} Alright Meadows Crew, Listen up! It's time to get these trucks rolling out of here! Ok, Richard! You go with truck #1 (265). Lavis you're rolling with truck #2 (398). Kym you got truck #3 (416). Brandon you go with truck #4 (561). Samantha truck #5 (624). George your riding with truck #6 (721). Rachel you with truck #7 (834). Last, but not least. Porshia truck #8 (959). When you guys reach your destinations. You will be greeted by the warehouse managers on site. He or she will give each of you two things. One; a form to bring back to me. Two; a set of car keys to the vehicle you'll be driving back with. Alright, you have your assignments. Meadows Crew, take your positions! It's time to roll out! I Will contact you guys by closed circuit CB's not by cell phones! Because all calls are recorded and documented. So, everything is by closed circuit conversations. Be safe, and I will see you guys tomorrow afternoon.

{The crew replied} Yes sir!

{Richard} Here we are in Maryland. How much further we got to go?

{Anthony} About another 10 miles, and we'll be there shortly.

{Richard} Good! We all left Pearson's Dock around 3am.

{Anthony} I know right, but don't worry we're almost there.

{Samantha} I wonder if the others reached their destinations?

{Tyrone} Huh, I doubt it! 3 of them had to go farther than we do. Unless they were speeding.

{Samantha} They better not be speeding! Mess around and get caught, then just stick a fork in their ass!

{Tyrone} Why!?!

{Samantha} Cause they're done!

{Tyrone} Damn! I guess so. By the way, how much stuff is we hauling anyway!?!

{Samantha} How does 7.5 million worth of supplies per truck sounds to you?

{Tyrone} Got Damn! Per truck!?!

{Samantha} Yes! Per truck.

{Tyrone} Umm! Umm! Umm! That amount x 8 = $60 million total!
{Samantha} You got it Einstein!

{Lavis} We'll I'm glad we've made it.
{Mark} Yep! We're here, and not a moment too soon.
{Lavis} Well, Paul should be contacting us soon. I wonder if he contacted the others?
{Mark} More than likely he did. Paul don't want to hear anything going wrong.
{Lavis} You better believe it! Let me get the manager, so I can get the hell back.
{Kym} Hey Paul, look we made the delivery. I'm getting ready to be back on my way home. Did you contact the others?
{Paul} Some of them I did, and some; not yet!
{Kym} Ok Samantha just got there a few minutes ago. George is on the dock unloading. Rachel is on her way back. Porshia texted me saying Everything is everything!
{Paul} Ok Lavis is tightening up down there. Richard is on his way back, and George is also on his way back.
{Kym} Well mission accomplished. Ha-Ha! I guess the Shepherd is waiting for his lost sheep!?!
{Paul} Yes! I am.

CHAPTER 3

No More Snitches

That's How You Handle Business

{Kym} Ok Paul, now that the crew is returning to base. We can get things going.

{Paul} Yes, operation is in full effect. I must with meet Mr. Montego. You know he pretty much run things on the south end of Washington D.C.!

{Kym} Damn FED town!

{Paul} Yep! FED Town it is. Nothing more than the local Boss in town.

{Kym} Wow, well how much supplies he's looking to get, or shall I say . . . purchase.

{Paul} Oh about $250,000 worth. He got the guns, but he's going for the fine china and snow!

{Kym} Got Damn! That's a lot of supplies.

{Paul} Yeah, but he can handle the weight! Ah yes, the crew has returned.

{Richard} Yep! We're back, and all drops has been made. Ha-ha! Look at Brandon, rolling up in here like he's King Tut!

{Brandon} Oh yes . . . It's good to be back home! So now we're all here, what's next on the menu to do!?!

{Now everyone's returned to base, but Porshia is still in route}

{Paul} Well it's all about sales; sales; and more sales. Always monitoring the areas where you guys made the drops at!

{Samantha} Everything is going well, and I'm pretty sure no one wants to cross us!

{Paul} Damn straight! Cause if they do, they through! Time for a Disappearing Act!

{Rachel} Hey what's going on with you guys!?!

{Paul} Good My platoon is here. Now I'm waiting on a call from Montego.

{Lavis} Oh yeah, Paul I need to have a word with you.

{Paul} Ok . . . We'll talk in my office.

{Kym} Porshia! Where have you been!?! You're the last of the Mohicans coming in here!

{Porshia} I know Kym; I know! Heck, we had to travel the farthest, but I made it back.

{Kym} Yeah! Thank goodness you made it back.

{Porshia} Girl let tell you! That was a heck of a ride!

{Kym} Well, what happen?

{As Porshia explains her trip to Kym. Lavis is telling Paul about an employee, that's talking a little too much!

A New Piece of Information

{Paul} Alright Lavis, what's on your mind?

{Lavis} I just got the word that, one of our employees is talking a little bit too much. About certain things going on in our operation.

{Paul} What the Hell you talking about Lavis!?! None of the employees knows, or even have a clue about our operations!

{Lavis} Yeah, I bet you differ! The employee's name is Daniel, and he's under Porshia's team.

{Paul} You don't think others are talking . . . Do you?

{Lavis} Not necessarily, because most of them already know that . . . Snitches gets stitches!

{Paul} The Hell with stitches! More than likely, going to make someone disappear!

{Lavis} Oh well, Poof! Be gone!

{Kym} Hey Paul! It's Montego on the phone.

{Paul} Hello Montego, what's going on the Southside of town?

{Montego} Everything is good! Business as usual, but I need new steel, so what do you have in your category of steel?

{Paul} Whatever you want I can get it.

{Montego} I know that's right! Well I'm looking for true steel. Not that ordinary stuff on the street.

{Paul} Oh ok . . . you want the Big Guns huh!?!

{Montego} You got it Paul, and nothing less!

{Paul} Alright! I will contact you tomorrow, and let you know. When my next steel shipment comes in.

{Montego} Alright Paul, be expecting to hear from you tomorrow.

{Paul} Sure thing, no later than 8pm.

{Montego} Good deal!

{Paul} Hey Uhm! Lavis and Richard, I need to see the two of you in my office.

{Richard} Ok what's going on?

{Lavis} Well Rich, I was just telling Paul that we might have a problem.

{Richard} What kind of problem do we have? And is it serious!?!

{Paul} I'm afraid so! Very serious! Lavis has brought to my attention. That one of Porshia's workers is running off at the mouth.
{Lavis} Wait a minute, we need to have Porshia in on this discussion.

A Leak in The Barriers

{Paul} Hello Porshia! Come on in and have a seat. Porshia you know I really appreciate everything that you do for our organization, right?

{Porshia} Yes, I know that!

{Paul} And you know that; we don't have time nor the space for careless mistakes, right?

{Porshia} So Paul . . . what are you getting at? I mean, what's really going on!?!

{Paul} Already! Someone in the organization is running off at the mouth, and the one is in your group.

{Porshia} Who is it then?

{Lavis} It's Mr. Daniels

{Porshia} Oh really!?! Are you sure Lavis?

{Lavis} Unfortunately yes. You see, I've gotten the word that Mr. Daniels has been talking about the shipment to different people in the warehouse. In which it's none of their business.

{Paul} So you know what we got to do, right Porshia!?! I guess we got to make an example out of someone. Talk too much about the wrong thing, to the wrong person, and things can take a wrong turn, for the worst!

{Porshia} Damn Daniels! Why!?! Well look, let me handle this! I will take care of this situation.

{Paul} You better!! Or you'll be going in his place! Don't think that you're not irreplaceable! You better make Daniels go To the left! To the left! I want Daniels ass buried to the left! Before I have ta' bury your ass to the right!! You understand where I'm coming from Ms. Porshia!?!

{Porshia} I hear you loud and clear Mr. Meadows.

{Paul} Very good! Now how are you aiming to handle this situation!?!

{Porshia} Well how about a DBA?

{Lavis} Yeah, but don't you think that's a bit messy?

{Paul} No, not necessarily. Because no castaway will perish on homeland grounds. Which means, they'll disappear in Foreign lands. DBA huh!?! Not a bad idea!

{Porshia} Me and Rachel will set it up. Paul, just get your pilot ready to take flight.
{Paul} I'm on it! I'll give Shawn a call right now!
{Richard} Who's Shawn?
{Paul} He's the pilot, and he works for me. A great connection in a high place.

DANIEL'S LAST SUPPER

{Porshia} Hey Samantha, I need you to do me a favor.

{Samantha} What's that?

{Porshia} I need you to get in contact with Mr. Daniels.

{Samantha} Isn't he one of your workers!?!

{Porshia} Yes! It's time for the setup! He has a mouth that won't quit.

{Samantha} Oh really!?!

{Porshia} Yeah unfortunately, so I told Paul I'll handle it. I mean like, Already!! Talking about something you know nothing about!?! That's the shit that will get you killed!

{Samantha} Don't worry girl, I got you on this assignment.

{Samantha calls Daniels for the dinner arrangement.}

{Samantha} Well hello Mr. Daniels, and how are you this afternoon?

{Daniels} I'm fine, and you Samantha. So . . . what do I owe for the pleasure of this call?

{Samantha} Oh nothing, I'm calling you on behalf of Porshia's request.

{Daniels} Porshia's request!?!

{Samantha} Yeah you see; she wants to meet with you, as a matter of fact . . . Well

I shouldn't say anything about it, but it's a surprise!

{Daniels} A surprise!?! Well what is it!?!

{Samantha} Oh alright, but don't let on that I told you anything about it!

{Daniels} Trust me, I won't say anything about the surprise. My lips are sealed.

{Samantha} Ok look . . . she's taking you on a romantic flight dinner! Now you can't say anything about the flight dinner. Just let it happen.

{Daniels} Hey, I got it! I got it! But uh, what did I do to deserve this Special Treatment!?!

{Samantha} She's been hearing a lot about you. You know . . . your work ethics, and how good you are about holding information. She will call you on the details of the date.

{Daniels} Ok, sounds good. Good bye!

{Samantha} Yeah Bye! Well Mr. Daniels, this will be your last date! Now let me get Porshia on the phone. Hello . . . Porshia, it's Samantha!

{Porshia} Well did you set it up with Daniels?

{Samantha} Hook; Line; and Sinker! He took the bait, now reel him in for the kill!

DANIEL'S FINAL MEAL TICKET

{Samantha and Porshia's plan are in motion. To perform one of the greatest acts in the world To make a man, Disappear!}

{Porshia} Hello Mr. Daniels, how are you? This is Porshia.

{Daniels} Well Hello Porshia, I've been waiting on you! For your call so what's going on?

{Porshia} I've been hearing good things about you, at the warehouse. I also been noticing your work ethics. So, to show our appreciation for all your work, and dedication. I'm personally inviting you for a flight dinner.

{Daniels} A flight dinner?

{Porshia} Yes..... To show you our appreciation and gratitude, for the work you do for this company.

{Daniels} Well is this business, or personal?

{Porshia} Both! business for the boss, and personal for me. I will pick you up in an hour. Oh yes, dress casual! I love that in man!

{Daniels] Your wish . . . Is my command, Madam!

{An hour goes by, and then the doorbell rings.}

{Porshia} Good evening Mr. Daniels. Are you ready for this evening?

{Daniels} Why yes Madam! I am ready!

{Porshia} The pilot will meet us at the airport, but we're going by limo. This is going to be a night to remember!

{After the limo ride, and then entering the jet. To encounter they're Flight Dinner.}

{Daniels} I don't remember the last time; that I had a great meal like that!

{Porshia} Oh I'm so glad that you enjoyed your meal. Oh Uh . . . Stewardess!

Drinks please!?!

{Daniels} Oh my goodness; I couldn't eat another thing! I'm stuffed.

{Porshia} Oh don't be silly, it's just a toast to celebrate!

{Daniels} Oh ok, There's no belly harm in that! Ha-ha!

{Porshia} Of course not. Well Daniels, here's to you! A merit of success! Now Rachel!{As she injects knock out serum into his neck.}

{Daniels} What the Hell . . . Is . . . Going . . . On?

{Rachel} Ok Porshia, he's fast asleep. Now what to do with him?

{Porshia} Are we're over the mark that was instructed?

{Shawn} Yes, we're approaching the target!

{Porshia} Ok George! You can come out and help Rachel to dump this fool out the plane, and into the Den of Hyenas!

{George} Damn this is cold!

{Porshia} Oh well! Handle that and toss the Damn Fool like a Caesar Salad!

{Rachel} The door is engaged to be opened George! And we're over the mark!

{Porshia} Drop him now!

{At that moment, Daniel vaguely opened his eyes.}

{Daniel} Hey! Hey! What the Hell are you guys doing!?! LET ME GO! No! No!

{Rachel} Enjoy the meal fellas! Well stick a fork in that ass!

{George} Why!?!

{Rachel} Cause he's Done!

{Porshia} Shawn! Return to base. Mission accomplished!

{Rachel} You're about to let Paul know what happened?

{Porshia} Most definitely, I'm calling him now! Hello Paul . . . This is Porshia. Everything's taken care of. Oh, by the way; Daniels really enjoyed his Final Flight Dinner.

{Paul} He did?

{Porshia} Why certainly . . . It was a Great Meal Ticket!

CHAPTER
4

THE HEAT IS ON!

THE DAY AFTER

{Paul} Well Richard . . . Mr. Daniels is a Done Deal, or shall I say . . . A Great Meal Ticket!

{Richard} So . . . Rachel and Porshia done handled the situation dealing with the motor mouth!?!

{Paul} Yes! They did, but those loose lips sank his own ship, and here comes Samantha.

{Samantha} Hello fellas; beautiful day isn't it? No more loose lips huh!?!

{Richard} Nope the hole has been plugged.

{Paul} Now everybody come and look at this . . . sales are up in Maryland! We're already at 60% of a turnover.

{Samantha} What about Delaware, Philadelphia!?!

{Paul} Sales are going well in those areas also. Virginia is eating it up, sales are at 70% . . . Washington D.C. aka Chocolate City . . . they're at an all-time high! Sales are at 85%. Damn!

{Kym} Sales! Did I hear the magic word? Sales!

{Richard} Yes you certainly did. Even though, you missed the numbers of percentage. The numbers are up!

{Paul} Yes! Everything is going well in those areas.

{Kym} What about the Metropolitan area?

{Paul} Oh . . . You didn't get the memo!?! The weather man predicted heavy snow in the metro. As a matter of fact, a major blizzard is roaring through! It's going to freeze the N.Y.C.; Connecticut; and New Jersey!

{Porshia} Well Paul, we're back!

{Rachel} And not a moment too soon. Almost feel jetlagged!

{Paul} I wonder where George and Brandon are!?!

{Porshia} Well I spoke to Brandon not to long after we got off the plane. George said he'll be here shortly. Hey Richard, how's your wife doing?

{Richard} Patricia, she's good! Thanks for asking.

{Rachel} When was the last time, you seen her?

{Richard} This morning, even though it seems like I'm always at work, but believe me! I Always . . . Go Home!

Business as Usual

{George} Alright Paul I'm here now, so what's going on?

{Paul} Ok we're going to take a trip this weekend.

{George} Where are we heading to!?!

{Paul} We're going to Georgia!

{George} Sweet Georgia huh!?! We must be taken on new markets.

{Paul} You got it man. Before you know it . . . We will have the entire East Coast on lockdown! Then start taking on all the Central parts, and then West Coast.

{Richard} Now Paul, you know you're moving too fast. Slow down . . . take your time!

{Paul} Hey now, wait a minute! I'm not moving too fast. We're moving according to our operations; as they are expanding. So that's why we're going to Georgia this Friday!

{George} Ok so, who's the contact person we suppose to meet down there?

{Paul} Kym! Enlighten us, of the contact person.

{Kym} Her name is Salena. She controls things down in the ATL, also Darlington, and Decatur. She really puts the Peach, in Georgia!

{George} I see, so what about checking the Metro areas!?!

{Paul} Don't you worry about the Metropolitan area. I got it all, on lockdown!

Nothing moves unless I give the cue!

{George} Alright then, now where's Lavis, and Brandon? It's not like them to miss a meeting before making moves.

{Lavis} I'm here George, I wasn't far at all. Just talking to Samantha in the other room, and Brandon is outside.

{Kym receives a call from one of the workers, from the warehouse.}

{Kym} Oh my goodness!

{Richard} What's wrong Kym!?!

{Kym} It's Jason from the warehouse. I hope everything is alright? Hello, Jason is everything alright!?!

{Jason} No because, one of the crates was left behind. I called the driver to come back to pick up the crate that was left.

{Kym} What's the number on the crate?

{Jason} 2680013 is the SKU, it's supposed to be heading to Portsmouth, VA.

{Kym} Don't worry, I will call the driver back and he will come back and pick it up.

New Markets; New Missions

{Brandon} Hey Richard! I hear that we're going to Georgia Friday afternoon.

{Richard} You heard right. My wife is getting on edge. About all the extra trips, extra-curricular activities I've been working on! If she had a clue, of what I've been up to with Paul. She'll have my head on a platter!

{Brandon} Well . . . I'm not married, but my sister is a worry ward herself. Like I tell her all the time. I must handle my business.

{Selena calls Kym}

{Selena} Hello Ms. Kym, how are you and the crew? You guys are coming down this Friday!?!

{Kym} Yes! Estimate time of arrival should be around 7 o'clock.

{Selena} Good! That'll be perfect timing. We'll be taking a tour around the area's I was telling you about.

{Kym} Very well. See you guys Friday evening.

{Lavis} Paul, I'm going now, and take of some business cross town. I'll be back in a little while.

{Paul} Alright, and uh . . . while you're out. Get in touch with Shawn and let him know about Friday's trip!

{Lavis} No problem, I'll take care of it.

{Lavis contacts Shawn about Friday's trip. Now the day has come, and the crew is ready to go.}

{Shawn} Well Paul we're ready to take off, and all systems go!

{Paul} Excellent! What you say my crew!

{Everyone replied, Georgia . . . Here we come!}

{Shawn} We should be landing in Georgia shortly.

{Kym} Good deal! Selena should be at the airport waiting on our arrival.

{Paul} Everything is going as scheduled. No loose ends here!

{Lavis} Hey Samantha, maybe we can get something to eat. After the meeting with Selena.

{Samantha} I like that, but first taking care of business is top priority. You know how it goes.

{Lavis} True indeed!

{Paul} Well were coming in for a landing. What's going on with you Richard?

{Richard} I don't know about this Paul. Something just don't set right with me, about the whole trip.

{Paul} Richard, I wish you would stop worrying! You know we're prepared for any type of emergency. We all strapped to the tee! Look, you let me worry about the moves we make, and you worry about everything going smoothly. Alright!?!

{Richard} Alright Paul! I got you.

{Paul calms Richard's nerves down. While Lavis is putting the moves on Samantha.}

{Lavis} So Samantha, what do you think about us as being a couple?

{Samantha} To tell you the truth Lavis. I never thought about us; being a couple. Being as which, we're crew members . . . more like family! But hey, I guess you got to start somewhere huh!?!

{Lavis} Sure you right!

{Richard} What are you two whispering about? Trying to be all Lovey-Dovey over there. Keep in mind that we're on business mode right now, not pleasure.

{Samantha} Come on now Richard! We're talking strictly business. All in the Kool-Aid, but don't know our Flavor!

{Lavis} Sure don't know our Flavor!

{Richard} Well that kind of flavor . . . I don't need to know about.

{Lavis and Samantha says at the same time} I know that's right!

{Richard} Ha-ha! Very funny! You guys should be in show business.

{Lavis} Why you say that?

{Richard} Because . . . The both of you be clowning.

{Samantha} Ha! You got jokes!

THE METHOD IN GEORGIA

{After landing the crew exits the plane and was greeted by Selena.}

{Kym} Hello Selena.

{Selena} Ms. Kym! It's a pleasure finally meeting the Infamous Meadows Crew!

So where is the rest of the crew?

{Kym} They're unloading the bags now. Ready to go to the hotel.

{Selena} Very well, my chauffeurs will take you all to the Radisson Hotel. I'm quite sure you will all be comfortable there.

{Kym} Oh yes! We certainly will be; very comfortable there.

{Kym phone rings, and it's Jason}

{Kym} Hello Jason, and how are things at the warehouse?

{Jason} Production is good, but we had a visitor.

{Kym} What visitor?

{Jason} A Detective by the name of . . . Holman! Came by and asking questions about Mr. Daniels. Saying that he's been missing for time now.

{Kym} Well you don't worry about that. Paul has everything under control. Cops and judges is on payroll. Oh, and Uh! Keep this under raptures until I return. No need to discuss this now, Kalpesh!

{Jason} Alright I'll chill! Playing it cool, but I hope he won't be snooping around. Look I will call you later. I must finish up, so I can go home, and relax.

{Kym} Ok bye!

{Paul} Hey Kym. Who was that you were talking to?

{Kym} Oh that was Jason! He called to inform me that we had a visitor.

{Paul} Oh really, what type of visitor!?!

{Kym} We'll talk when we get to the room later.

{Samantha} Now Rachel, you know Paul's expecting to go to the areas where the supplies and product are going to be distributed to.

{Rachel} I know Sam, but we got to take precautions. I don't trust this Selena trick as far as I can throw a building across the street. She looks like some Ole Itch Witch Snitch Bitch!

{Samantha} Ha-ha! You're funny Rachel! Well hey, we got to go with the flow. Besides . . . It's about getting paid right!?! We'll be rolling out in about an hour.

{Richard} Uh George! You got your heat on you?

{George} Damn straight I do! I don't have time for nonsense. You got yours!?!

In the Heat of Heat

{Richard} Yes Sir! Is everybody strapped!?!

{George} Supposed to be. No questions asked!

{Paul} Ok Kym, what visitor came by the warehouse!?!

{Kym} A Detective by the name of Holman, do the name ring a bell?

{Paul} No it doesn't ring a bell, but I want to know what he's looking for?

{Kym} According to Jason, he's been asking questions about Mr. Daniels Disappearance.

{Paul} Alright, I don't suspect he knows anything, and if he did! Good luck finding him! He won't be talking to anyone . . . anymore!

{Kym} He sure won't be talking about anything anymore! You can take that to the bank!

{Both Paul and Kym laughed}

{Lavis} Samantha look we got the room down the hall from everyone else.

{Samantha} What's wrong with that!?!

{Lavis} Well since you put it that way, I guess nothing's wrong. As a matter of fact, it's all good!

{Lavis and Samantha finds themselves kissing.}

{Samantha} Oh my! What just happened here?

{Lavis} Nothing but kissing!

{Samantha} Wow! Let's get ourselves together so we can get back and spend some quality time.

{Paul} Alright Richard . . . Let's get everyone together so we get to business. And we'll know how much supplies we need for the area's.

{Richard calls everyone to meet}

{Richard} Everybody's ready to roll out!

{Everyone replied} Yep!

{Selena} Ok Paul! Your crew is ready to see the area of Decatur, Atlanta, and Darlington.

{Kym} Yes! We're ready, let's go!

{Meanwhile back at the warehouse}

{DT. Holman} Yeah Chief, we're staking out the warehouse downtown. I'll call you when we got something.

{DT. Shultz} So Holman, what are we looking for at this warehouse?

{DT. Holman} Any suspicious activity. Trucks going in and out of the warehouse after hours. Things in that nature!

{DT. Shultz} Well what's going on here that we need to surveillance the area!?!

{DT. Holman} We have reason to believe, that a Mr. Daniels worked here at this warehouse; but suddenly he turns up missing. Disappeared without a trace, and no one knows what happened, or where he's gone to. Nothing! Just dropped off the face of the earth.

{DT. Shultz} Oh I get it! The reason to believe that Daniels disappearance is linked to this warehouse or shall I say who he worked for at this warehouse!?!

{DT. Holman} You got Shultz! The trouble is no one's talking!

{DT. Shultz} Well do you know who owns the building?

{DT. Holman} Well there's a guy named Jason. He's the assistant manager, but of course nothing from him neither.

CHAPTER
5
NEVER BACK DOWN

Standing on Shaky Grounds

{Paul} Richard! I need to have a word with you. Kym has informed me about a couple of detectives snooping around the warehouse. Asking questions about our friend, who had to take the plunge.

{Richard} Well Jason knows what to say, and what to do. Besides they just trying to find out his whereabouts.

{Paul} I know, but I know one thing for sure. If they get in the way of our operations. You already know what's going down right!?!

{Richard} Paul now wait! If you do anything to them, you'll be going away for life!

{Paul} Not necessarily. Keep in mind that I have connections in high places. No one wants to cross us. Remember, the line that we're walking it barely exist!

{Richard} Yeah, I know. The Invisible Line. Hey George, get the rest of the crew in here, so we can discuss about the amounts for each area.

{Meanwhile, Patricia is getting worried about Richard.}

{Patricia} Richard, where are you!?! You should be calling me. I haven't heard from him in two days! I got to call my husband! And see what's going on with him, and Paul!

{Richard phone rings}

{Richard} Hello . . . Oh Hi honey, and how are you love?

{Patricia} Richard, it's been two days! I haven't seen nor heard from you since then! Now what the Hell is going on Richard!?!

{Richard} Nothing sweetie. Nothing's going on! Just taking care of business with Paul at the warehouse.

{Patricia} Well why are you so distant suddenly? Did you forget that you're a married man?

{Richard} No dear! I didn't forget . . . Look I will be home in the morning.

{Patricia} In the morning!?! So . . . where are you now, exactly!

{Richard} On my way home from Georgia! The crew is all together with Paul.

{Patricia} Okay, I will talk to you when you get home. Prayerfully you still have a home to come to!

{Richard} Alright! Alright! I will see you in the morning! Love you my dear.

{Patricia hangs up aggressively!}

{Paul} Wow! Is everything alright at home?

{Richard} Yeah everything's ok. Wifey is upset, because I've been gone too long.

No Pain; No Glory!

{Lavis} Well Rich, it seems like you're in the doghouse. How much is that doggie in the window? Ruff! Ruff!

{Richard} Lavis, I'm going to tell you one time; and one time only! Shut the Hell up! And I approve this message.

{Lavis} Alright Richie Rich . . . You don't have to be so touchy! Besides it's not my fault that you need to spend more quality time with your wife.

{Kym} That's right Richard! You got to tighten up when it comes to home.

{Richard} True that. When we get back, I'll be spending more time with my wife.

{Samantha} We should be arriving home about 7:45pm at the airport.

{Kym} Now that we're getting Georgia on lockdown. How many states we have now Paul!?!

{Paul} At approximate of nine states, and we're expanding our territories.

{Rachel} Ok Kym, who are the ones we supply?

{Kym} Gun shops; Pharmaceutical companies; and Major dealers.

{Kym phone rings, and it's Jason}

{Kym} Oh! Hang on for a second Rachel . . . Hello!

{Jason} Hey Kym; it's Jason. The Damn DT's are back! Snooping around again!

{Kym} Alright! Which one is close by you?

{Jason} Holman is right by me.

{Kym} Ima put Paul on the phone. When I do; put that bitch on the phone! Understand! Here Paul, phone for you . . . Damn detectives!

{Jason} Yes Ma'am! Holman, it's for you!

{DT Holman} Detective Homan, and who am I speaking with, as if I gave a damn!

{Paul} You have the grand pleasures of speaking with Mr. Paul Meadows, and you need to give a damn! If you and your partner still want your jobs!?!

{DT Holman} Now Paul, I know you know better than that! To be threatening a detective. Like are you serious!?!

{Paul} Yes! I'm very serious! Now I insist, no matter of fact I warn you!

{DT Holman} No Got Dammit I'm warning you! This is an official Missing Persons Case, and prayerfully, not to turn out to be a Homicide Case! Now if I were you, I would tread very lightly, like living by land mines. I do mean LIGHTLY!

A New Level of Uncertainty

{Paul} Look Detective . . . Whatever your name is? I have business to tend to, so if you don't mind, I must say . . . Good Bye!

{George} Now Paul! How in the world can you talk to a detective like that, and not to expect any repercussions from that!?!

{Paul} Pure elementary dear George! First, I told you guys a little while back. That I have many connections in high places. Now do you honestly believe, that I would be talking shit to a cop; detective; or whatever without being able to back up what I say!?!

{Kym} You got that right!

{Richard} You know it!

{Samantha} That's right Paul!}

{Lavis} True facts Paul!

{Rachel} I'm in full agreement with you Paul!

{George} Well in that case, there's no need to question the authority!

{Paul} Damn straight! If you're caught in the wrong, dammit you're wrong! Am I right?

{Everyone replied} You're right Paul!

{Paul} Wow through all the excitement, we're back home troops!

{Richard} Good! Now I can go home to my wife. To get things right at home.

{Kym} I know that's right Richard!

{Paul} Yeah Richard, you go home and spend quality time with your wife. The rest of us can handle, what we need to handle.

{Brandon} Ok Paul, now what you have in mind for the cops. Snooping around the warehouse.

{Paul} I'm going to get in touch with the Commissioner. He'll get in touch with their superior officer and see to it that they will not be coming back.

{Samantha} I know Porshia need to be getting in contact with us.

{Rachel} Yeah! Some PG she's turning out to be.

{Kym} Now you guys just wait a minute. Hold up the Hell up! Porshia's our girl! How can you stand there and say things that!?!

{Paul} That's right . . . when we need her she's right there, and I don't ever want to hear that kind of smut again about any of our crew members. Do you ladies understand me!?!

{The ladies replied} Yes sir!

{Kym} He's right! In unity there's strength.

{Samantha} We know Porshia is cool with us, but she needs to be present more.

{Porshia} Ok I'm here now! What's going on!?!

{Paul} Hello Porshia, what's going on is that, we have new markets going on in Georgia. No matter what we face, we will conquer and control the market! Nothing can hold, nor stop The Meadows Crew now!

Meadows Crew Tightens Up

{Richard} Patricia I'm home! Honey where are you?

{Patricia} Thank GOD!! You're home! I haven't seen you in two days.

{She smacks Richard across the face and asks.}

{Patricia} Where the Hell have you been!?! That you can't call me! They have made phones where you can see the person you're talking to.

{Richard} Yes babe, I know. Skype and all other types of vision phones are in effect. Look I know I should've called, but time waits for no one. I'm sorry! I will be calling you, especially when I'm going to be late.

{Patricia} Ok Richard! For now, on call me; and let me know what's going on! Now after dinner you and I got some Business to attend to!

{Richard} What business?

{Patricia} My body business! Do I make myself clear Mister!

{Richard} Yes! Your wish is my command my lady!

{George} Ok Paul I'll go and check out the warehouse. While you talk to the Commissioner.

{Paul} Good idea! If you come across those detectives. Call me ASAP! Don't talk to them, or anything! Just call me.

{George} You got it Paul.

{Paul contacts the Commissioner}

{Paul} Hello Commissioner. It has been long time, since we last spoke Commissioner Smith.

{G. Smith} Well hello Paul. Nice to hear from you again. Yes! it has been a long time. So, my friend, what's going on? How's the real estate business treating you?

{Paul} Oh everything's going well, but I don't know why that . . . Two of your DT's Is always snooping around my warehouse.

{G. Smith} Are you serious Paul!?!

{Paul} Yes! Unfortunately, I am very serious, and it would be greatly appreciated if you could stop them from harassing my establishment.

{G. Smith} Don't worry about it. Paul. I will take care of it!

{Paul} Thanks good buddy! I knew I could count on you.

{G. Smith} No problem! Anytime.

{Kym} Samantha, Porshia, and Rachel listen up!

{They replied} Yeah Kym what's up!?!

{Kym} Alright ladies listen up! Paul has given me the word. That we got to go and make sure that the trucks arrive on time at the warehouse.

{Samantha} What time they supposed to be arriving there!?!

{Kym} By 8pm, so we better get moving.

Accommodate & Consolidate

{As the ladies arrive to the warehouse}

{Rachel} I know we got to secure the area, and our supplies.

{Kym} Most definitely! Do whatever we got to do! To make sure that these trucks get the stuff and deliver to their appointed destinations.

{Porshia} Ok Kym, where are the trucks? It's 8:25 and they're not here yet!

{Kym} Relax ladies, they'll be here shortly.

{The sounding of trucks pulling up outside.}

{Rachel} Well Kym you were right. They're here now.

{Kym} Alright Samantha, get Brandon and George on the phone so they can get over here.

{Samantha} Will do.

{Samantha calls Brandon}

{Brandon} Hey Sam, what's going on?

{Samantha} Look Brandon the trucks are at the warehouse. Can you and George get over here soon as possible?

{Brandon} Yeah, no problem! As a matter of fact, George is with me now, so we're on our way.

{Samantha} Good, see you guys when you get here.

{Lavis} Nowadays you can't trust Richard! So, you mean to tell me that you fully trust Paul!?!

{Richard} Lavis, I have trusted Paul with my life! So far, I have not been disappointed by Paul. Now what's your issue with him?

{Lavis} Richard I'm telling you man, something just not setting right with me about Paul.

{Richard} Well if that's the case, why you still down with the program? Since you don't have a good feeling about Paul. Just back the hell out of it all!

{George; Brandon; and Paul arrives at the warehouse.}

{Paul} Well I see most of the crew is here. Now where's Rich and Lavis?

{George} None of us spoke to neither one of them today. When the last time you spoke to them?

{Paul} Earlier with Richard, but let's get these trucks packed with these shipments. We got crates of steel, and crates of snow to go.
{Kym} Don't worry about the books Paul. Everything is lined up for taxes. All supplies are linked to the electronics, school supplies, and fabrics. All the steel, are going to the gun shops throughout Georgia.
{Paul} Great! I had a talk with the Commissioner, and I believe we've seen the last of our detective friends; snooping around here.

CHAPTER
6

No Sparing Love 4 Business

Time to Turn up the HEAT!

{Kym} So you had a talk with Commissioner Smith. I hope those detectives won't be back around here.

{Paul} Yes, I certainly did! We don't have to worry about Abbott and Costello lurking around here anymore.

{George} Hey Samantha, where's Porshia? I know she's got be around here somewhere?

{Porshia} I'm over here George. Damn, did you miss me!?!

{George} Yeah, I did but I thought you might've left again. Like poof, your gone!

You fit the title, of an old favorite movie of mine. You know . . . Disappearing Acts.

{Porshia} Ha! ha! Oh, I see you got jokes, huh George!?!

{Paul} Alright guys enough with the Comedy Central. We to get these trucks loaded, and ready to roll out by 5 in morning. And where the hell is Richard and Lavis!?!

{Samantha} Ok Paul, I will call them; and get them over here.

{Samantha} calls Lavis}

{Lavis} Hello Samantha, how are you?

{Samantha} Hello Lavis, Is Rich with you now?

{Lavis} Yep! He's here!

{Samantha} Look . . . you guys need to get to the warehouse as soon as possible! We have the shipments going out in the morning 5 to be exact!

{Lavis} Alright. We'll be there shortly.

{Samantha} Good! The sooner the better. Especially for you Lavis!

{Lavis} Why you say that!?!

{Samantha} When we're finished . . . then you'll find out!

{Lavis} Richard! Time to go!

{Lavis and Richard arrives at the warehouse.}

{Paul} Well, it's all about time you guys got here! I was wondering if you guys would make it, or not.

{Richard} Now you know we was going to make it! Just running a little behind schedule though.

{Rachel} Yes! More help, now the trucks will get out of here on time.

{Samantha} Uh Lavis! You need to come with me. We can do so much more!

{Kym} Alright you two! Don't go disappearing in the night. We got work to do! Truck loading work! Not each other's body work . . . Kalpesh!

New Level of Motivation

{It is now 4:30 am, and the trucks are loaded}

{Paul} I love it when a plan comes together!

{Richard} So Hannibal Smith! Are you proud of your A-Team?

{Paul} Yes, so you're Face, and you can go tell B.A. Barracks and Murdock. To come into the upper room!

{Richard} I guess you're referring to George and Brandon.

{Paul} You got it Rich! Oh, and duh! By the way . . . Call your wife.

{Richard} Most definitely!

{Meanwhile Samantha, and Lavis are having they own celebration.}

{Lavis} Sam, I'm so glad we're finished these trucks. Now we can have our time.

{Samantha} Yes! Now bring your delicious; snack looking, self over here to me right now!

{Richard} You two, go get a room!

{Lavis} Rich my man . . . were you standing there watching us?

{Richard} No thanks! I got my own Rated x show that I can watch and participate in thank you very much! And by the way, where's George and Brandon? Paul wants to see them before they leave.

{Samantha} They outside talking to the drivers. I'll go get them.

{Samantha} Hey George, and Brandon! Paul wants to see you guys before you leave.

{Brandon} Come on George we got to go see the boss man before he has a fit.

{George} Ha-ha! You are so crazy Brandon.

{Kym} Well ladies, I guess the trucks are ready to go! Another successful evening of loading up the trucks!

{Rachel} Yes ma'am! All's well that ends well!

{Porshia} Good deal! Hey Kym, do you think those cops will come back!?!

{Kym} I don't think so! Why you ask?

{Porshia} I don't know, it's always calm before the storm! And oh yeah, it's been too Damn calm!

{Kym} Well according to Paul. He's had a talk with the Commissioner about the problem. I'm sure it's been taken care of!

{As the Meadows Crew leaving the warehouse. They are being greeted by some unwelcoming guest}

{DT Holman} Well hello to Paul and the crew! It's so nice to see you guys again!

{Paul} Detective Holman . . . But I'm not going to say the same for you. So, what may I do for you?

{DT Holman} Don't think for one solitary moment that this investigation is over. humph, not by a long shot. In fact, It's only the beginning.

{Paul} Oh yes! It was declared over when I talked to the Commissioner. You know the boss that's over your boss! You better stand down and obey your Commander in Chief! The H.N.I.C! You know what that spells, don't cha!?!

If You Want Some;
Come Get Some!

{DT Holman} Yes, I know what it spells, but like I said Paul This is not over by a long shot, so get used to seeing this face. Cause it's going haunt you like a phantom at Halloween.

{Paul} You know Holman, you talk more shit than a little bit! You will have to show me better than you can tell me!

{Richard} Hey Paul! Look man, we don't have time to be going back, and forth with some two-bit half breed of a cop.

{DT Holman} Ha! You know what . . . Your whole crew, is getting ready to go down. The question is: When, and where!?! Huh! Don't need to ask why!

{Paul} Well my questions are as follows: One. Why are you still here, talking a bunch of nonsense to me? Two. When will you guys realize that; you can't touch The Meadows Crew! Unless I give you permission to. And I did not! Grant you any wishes; or permission to do so! And the hell with where! Ha! Because You guys, are out of your league! Now get back there; where you belong!

{DT Holman} I am not to be put off like some . . .

{At that moment; Kym interrupts the whole conversation.}

{Kym} Look dammit! You are the weakest link, Goodbye!

{Lavis} I know that's right Kym!

{Richard} Oh shit, we can go home now!

{DT Holman} Ok Meadows Crew, you all may be laughing now! But I promise each, and everyone of you. It's not over until I say, It's over!

{Paul} Well Dammit say over! Because it is, now Goodbye!

{Samantha} Look Lavis, you are coming with me to my place, and that's final!

{Rachel} Like damn, how long them two been arguing? About when we are supposed to get busted!?!

{Brandon} We're going home Meadows Crew! Rachel, you down for breakfast at Denny's!?!

{Rachel} Sure why not! Paul, and Holman done argued me up an appetite! Damn I'm starving!

{Richard calls home.}

{Richard} Hey honey; what are you doing?

{Patricia} Nothing much, where are you?

{Richard} Just leaving the warehouse. Paul was arguing with the Detective, Ha! Funny to me.

{Patricia} What the Hell is wrong with Paul!?! Acting a fool! Mess around, and have his mouth write a check that his ass can't cash!

{Richard} Ha-ha! Don't worry baby, Paul has it all under control. He done called the Commissioner about them harassing us!

{Patricia} Richard honey, tell me something. What do Paul have you doing for him!?! I mean really? Are you guys doing something illegal?

{Meanwhile, Samantha and Lavis are planning their evening.}

{Samantha} Oh my goodness, I'm so glad that we finally got away from the warehouse! Damn, let Jason and his co-workers handle that.

{Lavis} I know babe, but don't get comfortable. You know the minute we do. There goes the phone! You'll be like dammit not now!

{Samantha} Well Lavis, we're finally alone, so you know the Old' saying, "If you want some . . .

{Lavis} Come get some!

{Samantha} Oh and uh, believe me Lavis. I'm just going to uhm . . . Take me some of you!

{Lavis} Well don't talk about it; be about it and bring it on!

New Method for the Madness

{Detectives Holman, and Schultz Working on a new plan of operation.}
{DT Schultz} Ok we only got shot at cracking the missing persons case of Mr. Daniels. Who worked for Mr. Paul Meadows.
{DT Holman} Yes! One shot, and one only! Which is not going to be easy. Being that he called the Commissioner on us.
{DT Schultz} We better be careful. Paul has higher ups on his payroll. Ok, so beware of the favoritism! That's in his favor.
{DT Holman} But, sooner or later. That ass is going to get caught! And I will make it my business . . . to catch that ass!
{DT Schultz} That's going to be a hell of a fight! You know his crew is military trained. I'm talking Marines style! I mean Hell Have you even looked at their background!?!
{DT Holman} Why yes, I have Schultz, and I brief you with their background facts!
{DT Schultz} Please do!
{DT Holman} Alright! Are sure you want to hear everything about the Meadows Crew!?!
{DT Schultz} Yes! I want to hear everything about them. No matter how ugly it can be and knowing how you are. Talking about going head to head with them! I need to know everything about Paul and his crew.

{DT Holman} Alright Schultz! I got their backgrounds right here, let's begin!
Paul Meadows aka "Meadows" age 45; Caucasian born in Nashville, TN. After High School he went into the Marines. Became a Drill Sergeant and moved up in the ranks to Green Beret's. Fought in Afghanistan, and leader of a special forces group! Meadow Seals Tactical Group. Specialties in Martial Arts; Special Weapons Trainer; Chemical Specialist; the man is a lethal weapon! Richard Miles aka Righthand age 41; African American born in Chattanooga, TN. He's Paul right side man! Also, a member of the Marines. His rank was soldier, but don't sleep on him. He might be mild mannered, but he's lethal too!

Specialist in Weapons; Bombs; 3rd Degree Black Belt in Tai Kwon Do and Archery Master. Next, we have Lavis Coltrane aka Links age 44; Caucasian. Born in Tampa Bay, FL. Seems that he had a rough childhood. His Mother got killed from a terrible car accident. And Lavis seen his Father got shot down in the street on Christmas Eve.

{DT Schultz} Damn! How old was Lavis when all this happened to his parents?

{DT Holman} Well when his Mom got killed he was 12, and he was 16 when lost his Dad. After that, he was placed in the system. Two different foster homes. When he turned 19 after graduation, Lavis went into the Marines. He ranked Drill Sergeant with the same special training as Richard, but I'm nowhere near done.

More Informative Information

{DT Holman} Okay let me see . . . Oh yeah, next in line we have George Matthews aka Gatz age 40; African American. Another Marine Corp who specialty is in Weapons. He's like the American Sniper! He never missed a target. If he gets you in his sights, well let me put it to you this way. If he does you're through!

{DT Schultz} Damn! Are you sure we're barking up the right tree!?!

{DT Holman} Yep I'm sure! Next, we have Brandon Wiley aka Butcher age 38; Mexican. Marine Corp Green Beret's! Believe me he's no short taker either! Specialist in Knives, Martial Arts 3rd Degree blackbelt Ninjutsu! He can hit a target square dead in the head. Stars; Knives; any kind of blade. At approximate 20 to 30 feet away. Oh, did I mention that, he's also a sharp shooter!?! I didn't! Damn I must've forgotten! Well that's all for the fellas! Now for the Ladies!

Kym Lei, aka Digits age 39; Asian American. Born in San Francisco, CA. College Grad with honors. Specialist in Accounting. Also, Marine Corp Wave. Specialist in Weapons; Tai Kwon Do; she looks sweet as Dove, but Deadly as a Viper! Samantha Hues aka Siren age 39 African American; Marine Corp Wave. Now she's the type; that can come up behind you and snap your neck into! Specialist in Bomb Expert; Special Weapons Trainer; and Chemical Specialist.

{DT Holman} Now we have Rachel Gaines aka PG1 age 38; Caucasian. Born in Greensboro, NC. After graduation, she went into the Marine Corp. Also, a Wave; she's very tactical too. No holds barred type! Lethal as the rest of them! Special Weapons; Bomb Expert; etc., etc. Last but certainly not the least, there's Porshia Brown aka PG2 age 39; African American born in Baltimore, MD. After graduation she went into the Marine Corp. She ranked as Sergeant, but she too got connected with Meadows Group, and she's no slow leak neither! Both Porshia and Rachel are the Point Guards in The Meadows Crew. They're a Militant Mob! A force to be reckoned with! You see Schultz. They're highly successful, so I don't understand why they would want to go crooked, and risk everything that they worked so hard for! It just doesn't make any sense!

{DT Schultz} Well one step at a time, and Holman. You better know what you're doing. Because if you don't, you have hell to pay!

{DT Holman} Well then, let the games begin!

{DT Schultz} So you saying, it's on Holman!?!

{DT Holman} Damn straight I am, and nothing further about it! Now you know. Who and what we're up against. Are in with me, or out!?!

{DT Schultz} Yeah, I'm in!

CHAPTER
7
There's No Love in War!

No Games on the Battlefield

{Paul calls for a meeting with the crew.}

{Paul} Hey Rich! Look get everyone together. Calling for an emergency meeting!

{Richard} Alright I get them together.

{Richard texts the crew for an urgent meeting with Paul}

{Lavis} See, what did I tell you Samantha! As soon as we get comfortable. That damn phone starts ringing!

{Samantha} I know, but we're going to take some time for ourselves!

{George} Ayo Brandon! We got an urgent meeting to attend to.

{Brandon} Well let's go!

{Kym} Okay! Rachel and Porshia. We have an important meeting to attend with Paul.

{Everyone meets at the warehouse.}

{Paul} Good afternoon Meadows Crew! Well the reason for this meeting is because of the Detectives that came to see me. Wants to take down the Meadows Crew!

{Richard} Well, they must really want Hell from The Meadows Crew! They must don't know why we're called Meadows.

{Paul} Yeah, but they truly going to find out; the real meaning! Won't they crew!?!

{The Crew responded} Yes sir!

{Kym} Paul, do we have to pull out the heavy guns for these two strumpets!?!

{Paul} No! Not yet, remember we don't war unless we must; but I got the strange feeling that Abbott and Costello are not going to let up!

{Rachel} Now you know they're not going to quit, so what's your plan of operation?

{Paul} Right now we got to be smart about everything we do. The shipments that just went out to Georgia. Are going to be distributed to the area's where we checked out.

{Lavis} Now what are we going to do, about the new incoming shipment? That one is at an approximate of 1.5 million! Due to arrive next Thursday around 4pm. At the aviation part of the airport!

{George} Yeah! A whole lot of freeze tag in that game.

{Porshia} Wow! Like Boys to Men sang at Christmas time, "Let It Snow!"

{Kym} Hey Paul What about that building you got the contract for!?!

{Richard} Yeah! You supposed to had started that project a couple of weeks ago.

{Paul} I know, I got that in the works, but as for the DT's are in concern. They better stay out of our way! If not, I'm gonna give them a tour that they will not come back from!

{George} Oh well! So that means, they must disappear too huh!?!

{Paul} I mean nothing more than that Kalpesh!

Drastic Times, Calls for Lethal Measures.

{Samantha} Kym . . . where are you and Rachel going to?

{Kym} Well right now we're heading to my office. I need to get some forms, so I can close this deal for Paul.

{Samantha} Ok Kym, you guys go and take care of that. Me and Lavis will stay here, and count inventory.

{Richard} Well Paul I'm going home! Time for me to get into some Meadows of my own.

{Paul} I know that's right bro! Tell Patricia I said hello.

{Richard} Will do.

{Meanwhile Detectives Holman and Schultz. Are plotting to takedown the Meadows Crew}

{DT Holman} I know that Paul had something to do with Mr. Daniels disappearance. I just can't prove it yet!

{DT Schultz} Well haven't you heard about Innocent, Until Proving Guilty!

{DT Holman} I have a serious hunch; my gut is telling me . . . that Paul did something to Mr. Daniels! And If my pit, is on point; and which I know it is! How did he do it? Where did he dispose of the body!?!

{DT Schultz} Are insinuating what I think you're insinuating . . . Murder!?!

{DT Holman} Did Paul kill Daniels, or had him killed? Shit! I smell foul play in the air, and with Paul . . . Bullshit is everywhere!

{DT Schultz} Like I said Holman . . . You better know what you're doing! Oh, damn there goes my phone again! Hold on, I got to make a call.

{DT Holman} Well, who you going to call!?!

{DT Schultz} Calling a connection to help us crack this case!

{Back at the warehouse, Paul gets a call from Lavis}

{Paul} Hello . . . Hey what's going on Lavis?

{Lavis} Any and everything that's not good.

{Paul} Alright! What's going on?

{Lavis} It seems that we have a problem in the VA area.

{Paul} What kind of problem are we facing in VA? Is it a financial problem, or a person's kind of problem!?! Meaning that we got to handle somebody!

{Lavis} Both! Thomas in West Virginia, and Simon in Newport News, VA!

{Samantha} What's wrong Lavis?

{Lavis} We got two bad wrinkles in VA. That we need to iron out! So, we won't take a loss in profits!

{Samantha} Oh really, so how you want to deal with this situation Paul?

{Paul} First off, I got to find out what's happening in those areas. Next, decide

On how to handle the situation.

{Samantha} Okay Paul. When you find out what you need to. Just let us know!

{Paul} I will, and it won't be long from now either! So be ready for anytime; anyplace; anywhere, and anyhow . . . It's going down!

{Samantha} We will Paul.

{Lavis} You know! I really starting to believe that it's going to get a little messy, bloody even! Oh well, when shit happens . . . Deal with it! Handle it as comes!

{Samantha} You're so right babe! It doesn't matter though. Our guns stay oiled and ready to spit fire! Hell, so bring it!

Clean Up Time in Virginia

{Paul makes a call to his contact.}

{Paul} Hey Montego this is Paul, what's going on in your neck of the woods?

{Montego} Nothing much, Business as usual. Got to keep things tight and right. So, what's good with you?

{Paul} Well; the way that I'm hearing about things, there's some wrinkles in your suit that needs some ironing out!

{Montego} Paul! What the hell are you talking about!?! Everything is good on this end.

{Paul} Yeah; are you sure about!?! It was brought to my attention that a Thomas in West Virginia, and Simon in Newport News. Has been messing up my business in those areas! Or shall I say, "Your Areas!"

{Montego} Oh really! Well this is the first that I'm hearing about this.

{Paul} Look Montego . . . Either you handle it, or I will! if I do It will not be pretty! Now I seriously advise you; to straighten this out pronto! Do I make myself clear!?!

{Montego} Don't worry about it Paul. I'll take care of it. As a matter of fact, do you want me to keep them, or lose them!?!

{Paul} Well Montego, I'm going to leave that up to you. Find out what's going on first! Then if they screwed up too much . . . let me know! Then it's time for a Houdini act!

{Montego found out what went wrong, so he calls Paul with the news.}

{Paul} Alright Montego. What did you find out?

{Montego} Well Paul you were right! About Thomas and Simon. They're both weak links. Now how do you want to handle this situation!?! Keep'em, or Lose'em?

{Paul} Montego you already know, that they got to go! I suggest that, you take care of it before I do.

{Montego} Don't worry Paul! They'll be taken out before the week's out, and as a matter of fact uh . . . Did you get that contract deal for that building yet?

{Paul} Ha-ha! Why yes, I did as a matter of fact; and I do believe that the building needs a fresh foundation. Catch my drift?

{Montego} I certainly do. In fact, I'm way ahead of you! So! We got to smooth out the lumpy and bumpy. In your new foundation tomorrow night at 8pm. I will be there, and so will Lumpy and Bumpy! Yeah there, and patiently waiting.

{Paul} Great! I will see you guys tomorrow night at 8. Well Kym Lei, I guess my building will be getting the foundation laid.

{Kym} When!?!

{Paul sings} Tomorrow! Tomorrow! I Love Ya! Tomorrow! You're Only A Day Away!

{Kym} Guess I'll be there as well!?!

{Montego} Yes you got to be there Ms. Lei. You don't want to miss out on all the fun do you!?!

Time to Layer the New Foundation

{Montego calls Thomas and Simon. For a Surprise Meeting}

{Thomas} Montego! What a surprise to hear from you. What can I do for you?

{Montego} Well I'm calling you, and Simon in for meeting. I would like for you to be at my office by 1 this afternoon. I will call Simon myself.

{Thomas} Alrighty then! I'll see you guys at 1.

{Montego} Hello Simon! This is Montego.

{Simon} Yes! I know so what's up Montego!?!

{Montego} Well I just got off the phone with Thomas. I'm calling for a meeting with you guys at 1pm this afternoon. At my office, now don't be late!

{Simon} No problem, I'll be there.

{Montego calls Paul to let him know, that the new foundation. Will be laid on time, as scheduled.}

{Paul} What's going on Montego? My foundation is on the way today!?!

{Montego} It will be there around 8pm.

The two contractors Lumpy and Bumpy, oh I meant Thomas and Simon. Shall be at my office at 1pm for the meeting. Then we'll be on our way.

{Paul} Sounds good! Well, see you guys at 8. Kym! Call Richard; Samantha, and Lavis. I want them at the Groundbreaking of the New Foundation. Oh, and uh. Tell Samantha to bring those knockout pills with her. I'm quite sure they'll come in handy.

{Kym} I'm sure they will!

{Montego} Welcome! I'm glad that you guys were able to make the meeting. Well Thomas and Simon, the reason for this meeting is more of a celebration.

{Simon} A celebration!?! For what?

{Thomas} Yeah! What are we celebrating?

{Montego} Promotion time fellas, and besides you guys are my top runners. Hey! We're heading to Nashville, TN. Tonight! We should be there around 8pm.

{Thomas} Ok . . . so what time we're leaving?

{Montego} Shortly around 3 o'clock.

{Now Montego; Thomas, and Simon are leaving for Nashville, TN. To meet Paul.}

{Montego} Hey Paul we're at the site, and it's 7:55pm. Where are you guys!?!

{Paul} Around the back. Where the tractors, and the cement mixer at. You guys come on, I'm sending my girl Samantha to meet you guys with drinks. By the way . . . you take the Gold trimming. They're glasses has their names on them!

{Montego} Fair enough! Fellas, let's go!

{Samantha} Well hello gentlemen! Glad you guys could make it to the Groundbreaking Ceremony. For the new foundation, so please take your glasses.

They have your names on them.

{They take up they're glasses, and toast to the Heavens.}

{Paul} Now Lavis, you know what to do when I give you the signal. Richard, you also know what to do.

{Lavis} For sure! I turn on the cement mixer, and let it pour.

{Richard} Yep, and I follow up with the John Deere. And compress their bodies in the cement. Hopefully crushing them, so they will move no more!

{Paul} Exactly right! Oh, here they come now! Welcome fellas to the Groundbreaking Ceremony.

{Montego} Paul, I like to introduce my guys. Thomas and Simon. Now it's time for the celebration!

{Thomas} Yes! It's time to celebrate! Why do I feel so sleepy?

{Simon} Yeah man me too! I'm yarning away like crazy.

{Kym} You got that right, and away you guys go!

{Paul gives the signal, and both Thomas and Simon fall face first in the hole of the foundation.}

{Paul} Ha-ha! Lavis and Rich follow up! Now this a Groundbreaking Ceremony we can build on! Ha-ha-ha-ha-ha-ha-ha-ha-ha-ha!
{Kym} Now that's Gangster Ladies and Gentlemen! Hell, now don't you forget it! Bye-bye! Bitches!

2 Down for the Price of 1.

{Montego} Well, that's that! Another one bites the dust, or shall we say . . . Two for the price of one.

{Paul} Yeah! We can also say the foundation is stabilized!

{Kym} I'm going to say it like this, Two down payments for the one New Up rise!

{Richard and Lavis said simultaneously} Damn that's cold!

{Samantha} Oh well! All's well; that ends well! So Lavis, my darling. I believe it's time to get back to what we were doing.

{Lavis} You're right babe. So, uh, we'll see you guys later.

{Paul} Certainly. See you guys tomorrow!

{Meanwhile Rachel and Porshia are meeting up with Brandon at his market.}

{Rachel} Hey Brandon, what's going on?

{Brandon} Hello Ladies . . . Nothing much going on right now. Just packing the meat in the freezer.

{Porshia} Well, Paul just had the Groundbreaking Ceremony a couple hours ago.

{Brandon} Oh! The foundation finally got laid?

{Rachel} Well you can say that the foundation is stabilized! Thomas and Simon from Virginia, was there. It was a celebration they'll never forget.

{Brandon} Or come back from! Oops! Did I say that out loud!?! Damn, poor Thomas and Simon. Well, they have no more worries!

{Richard calls his wife and plans for a romantic evening.}

{Richard} Hey honey! What are you doing?

{Patricia} Hey babe! I'm just relaxing. I'm a little tired, and I don't know why!?!

{Richard} Well babe, I was wondering if you wanted to catch a movie tonight!?!

{Patricia} Maybe another night, because I'm so tired tonight. I got to get some rest. I love you!

{Richard} Ok babe, I Love you too!

{Meanwhile, Detectives Holman and Schultz. Still at Paul's heels}

{DT Holman} You know what Schultz. I've been working on this missing person's case. Instead of trying to find out If Paul has been trafficking; racketeering. Any major shipments; Tax Innovation! Anything to make it stick to him, and his crew!

{DT Schultz} I hear you talking Holman, but you're looking for a needle in a haystack! Paul is not one of your local wannabe's. He's a business man, and if you're wrong I told you once before Holman. You could lose a whole lot more, than what you bargain for!

{DT Holman} Damn Schultz! Who side are you on? The good or the bad!?!

{DT Schultz} Now you know I'm on the good side. I'm just saying! You better know what you're doing. When you're dealing with Paul Meadows.

{Captain Harris walks in the office.}

{DT Holman} Well hello Captain Harris, and what can we do for you!?!

{Captain Harris} Look Holman, and Schultz. I come to let you guys know that, I'm taking you two off the Daniel's case. It will be at your best interest, not to be on this case.

{DT Holman} Oh come on Captain! Now you know . . .

{Captain Harris interrupts Holman}

{Captain Harris} Now that's an order detective! And no further discussion on the case. If I see; sense; or even smell your asses near this case. You guys will have to answer to me!

{DT Schultz} Captain why can't we . . .

{Captain Harris} I'm not up for the back and forth with you Schultz! Now is that clear detectives!?!

{Both Holman and Schultz answered simultaneously} Yes sir!

{Captain Harris} Alright! Carry on!

CHAPTER 8

PAUL MEADOWS, THE NEW DON

As the Sauce Thickens

{DT Holman starting to feel some kind of way about the law.}

{DT Holman} Hot Damn Schultz! No one around here wants to do what's right! seems like Paul Meadows got the police eating right out of the palm of his hands!

{DT Schultz} Well you see Holman . . . That's what I've been trying to tell you! Paul got a lot of pull around here. The Commissioner, which influences the Captain. And being as which, is enough to slow us down tremendously.

{DT Holman} You know what Schultz. I don't give a Damn! About how much pull Paul and his crew so called got.

{DT Schultz} You see Holman, that's where your overrating the whole thing. It's Paul! Who has all the connections. The crew wouldn't be as powerful without him.

{DT Holman} Well I'm ready to take his ass down right now! Come Hell, or high waters. It doesn't matter to me!

{DT Schultz} That's what it's going to be! If you call yourself messing with Paul Meadows! Trust me Holman, you're gonna have to let Paul make that fatal mistake. Because if you jump the gun too fast! Guess what!?! That's what you'll be having for dinner . . . A gun down your throat! Hell Bon Appetit!

{DT Holman} Well if that's the case Detective Schultz, how come he didn't make any jesters; or body language. For me to even insinuate, that he would do anything to me!?! Huh! Paul maybe Gangster, but he isn't stupid by far!

{Back at Paul's office. Richard, and Paul has a serious discussion about business.}

{Richard} Ok Paul, we got to get things tight and right. I hope you keep in mind, that every time make someone disappear. You going to get harassed more than before! Now just suppose those guys that we just buried. In which that are now part of the mixture of your buildings foundation. Has family that are looking for them right now!

{Paul} I hear you Richard, but so what!?!

{Richard} So what!?!

{Paul} Yes! So, what! It's not our fault they were messing up my business. If they we're handling business like they were suppose to. They wouldn't have had a Done Deal Disappearance.

{Richard} Paul! What are you doing!?! Man, you better stop; and think about how fast your ass is moving.

{Paul} Uh, Richard! I think I need to remind you of who the hell you talking to! First of all, I put you in charge as active supervisor over the crew. So, watch yourself Richard! You're my right-hand man. I trust you quicker than anybody else, but you know if you cross me . . . It's over! It's curtains for you, or anyone else for that matter goes!

{Richard} Okay, I see where this is going! So, on that note Paul! I'm going to say, goodnight. I'll talk to you tomorrow, but I will say this, you better watch your step my brother! Check yourself, before you wreck yourself! Cause bullets in your ass is bad for your health.

KYM GETS A NEW MEMO

{Paul pounders; on what Richard said!}

{Paul} Damn! Richard is my right-hand man, but now I'm starting to wonder. Do Rich really have my back, or not!?! I really need to get things together before everything starts to fall apart.

{Kym} Hey Paul! What's going on with Richard? He just flew past me like, if he had wings he could fly, and believe me . . . He did!

{Paul} No Kym! Everything's alright. He was just leaving for the day.

{Kym} Well ok, I just received a message from Montego.

{Paul} What did he say!?!

{Kym} Well I know you said; We will not war unless we have to . . . am I right Paul!?!

{Paul} That's right! So, what's happening?

{Kym} Well according by Montego, it looks like it's time for war.

{Paul} What the Hell, are you talking about Kym?

{Kym} Some local thugs from the Southside of Baltimore, are rivaling over sales and territories!

{Paul} Oh now I see! In other words, we have to make a special trip to the south side. For a little shakedown on these fools!

{Kym} It surely looks that way.

{Paul} Alright, you tell Montego that; if we come up there . . . it will not be a pretty scene! Hell, he better it together before we do.

{Kym contacts Montego and passes forward the message.}

{Montego} Now Kym, you guys know that I have no control over what these wannabe gangsters do out here. Let alone the Southsiderz!

{Paul} Who in Da' Hell are the Southsiderz!?!

{Montego} They're these local wannabees, that's trying to get a name for themselves.

{Paul} Yeah! A toe tag for each one of them! How many of them, and what are the ages?

{Montego} Mostly upper teenagers. Age ranges between 17 through 25! My guess about 15 of them total.

{Paul} Well in that case, I guess we can offer some ass spankings, and then send them home to their parents.

{Kym} All hell's about to break loose! Paul, you not about to war against some kids!?! That has no clue, about what we can do!

{Paul} No! I don't want to war against children, but they need to learn a lesson about staying in a child's place. Or shall I say, upper aged child's place.

{Kym} Paul! So, what are you going to do?

{Paul} Well, if you spare the rod . . . you'll spoil the child. So, no love in sparing the rod huh!?!

{Kym} Damn Paul! Kids included!

{Paul} Kym! Call Rachel and Porshia. I need some Motherly Love on these children, and uhm, oh yeah! Get George in on the fun too. Just in case they get a little besides themselves.

{Kym} LORD! Have Mercy!! So, George got to play poppa on them huh!?!

{Paul} Oh well! Shake; Rattle, and Roll the hell out on them, and I want this done before the week is out!

Sparing No Rods!

{Kym calls the PG's and George!}

{Kym} Hello Porshia, and I presume that Rachel is with you.

{Porshia} Yes, she is. What's going on!?!

{Kym} Well . . . Paul has another job for the four of us this time.

{Porshia} Which four?

{Kym} You, Rachel; George, and Myself.

{Porshia} Is Paul playing chess again?

{Kym} Yep! He certainly is. More so with children.

{Porshia} What!! Wait a minute! Hold up! Time! Freeze!! Children!?! What the hell is Paul trying to prove!?!

{Kym} Well I got a memo from Montego, and there's a bit of a problem. On the south end of Baltimore, MD.

{Rachel gets on the phone with Kym}

{Rachel} What kind of problems are there, on the south side?

{Kym} The Southsiderz! Some local wannabe gangsters from the south end. Ages 17 through 25.

{Rachel} So what are we suppose, to do with them!?! Read Mother Goose to these little hens! Send them to bed without supper? Oh! Oh! Oh! I got it! I got it! Put them on punishment and make them write 100 times on the black board. We will not act like Gangsters! Because we are somebody!

{Kym laughs at Rachel remarks.}

{Porshia} You crazy Rachel! But also mentioned that George must be with us as well. Damn! Do we really need Gatz with us? That's some heavy artillery right there.

{Rachel} True indeed Porshia. So, Kym why the heavy arsenal!?!

{Kym} Paul believes that, it's better to be safe than sorry. Especially dealing with local wannabees. Cause they're out to get a reputation for themselves, and they'll probably try to do anything to make that happen.

{Rachel} Got'cha! So, which one of us; is going to call George.

{Kym} You guys call, and fill George in; of what's going on! I got to make sure our trip is in place. Because Paul wants them handled before the week is out!

{Rachel} Ok. No casualties right!?! Just a spanking lesson!

{Kym} You got it Rachel!

{The ladies call George and fills him in on the situation.}

{George} I guess Paul wants us to sing them a lullaby song. Lullaby, and goodnight!

{Rachel} Stop it George! Nobody wants to hear you sing no lullaby!

{George} So, what do we do with our little league competition? Other than a shakedown!?!

{Rachel} Paul wants us to handle this situation before the week is out! Scare them so bad that, their pants will jump off their asses and run from them! Hell, they're halfway off anyway!

{Porshia} I have an idea that just might; do the trick.

{Rachel} And by what, pray tell do you have in mind?

{Porshia} Remember what we used to do to those who refused to talk, and to make them tell us what we wanted them to!?!

{George} Oh yeah The Old Tactical Routine.

{Porshia} That's right! Kidnap and take them to a dark place. Spotlight and Interrogate them!

{Rachel} I don't know if that's going to work with local hard heads.

{George} Well is Kym coming!?!

{Rachel} Yes, she is.

{George} Oh then it wouldn't be a problem putting them in check!

{Porshia} Damn straight!

{Rachel} Alright guys let's do this!

Lessons to be Learned

{Now that four of the Meadows Crew are gearing up for the trip. Paul has got to get the others to make moves for Georgia.}

{Paul} Great! You guys are ready to go to Baltimore and handle our minor problem.

{George} Don't you mean, Little League Fiasco!?!

{Rachel} George! Stop it now!

{George} Oh, I'm sorry! I almost forgot.

{Paul} Look y'all, this may seem like a bullshit assignment, but it's not! The Southsiderz has been problematic for some time now. At least a year!

{Kym} So we got to go and play vigilantes against these wannabees!?!

{Paul} Not so like vigilantes, but these guys have no respect for our territories.

{Kym} So, we got to show them the values of respect?

{Paul} Exactly Kym! You guys go and handle this matter. All I want to hear is Done Deal! Kalpesh!

{All answered} Yes Sir!

{Four of the Meadows, are leaving for Baltimore, MD. To rectify the problem on the Southside part of town.}

{George} I wonder what these Southsiderz going to be like dealing with?

{Kym} I don't know George, but what I do know is this . . . They better behave, or get that ass spanked! Yes! And you can take that; to the bank!

{Rachel} Believe that! I don't want to go out there. To spank somebody else's children, but business is business! So, when we get there; and let them know! What the real deal is . . . Hell! They better fly right or get thrown to the left!

{Porshia} Well, we shall see when we get there Huh!?!

{Meanwhile Richard and Patricia are having a discussion.}

{Patricia} Richard! Look I really would like to know. What you and Paul got going on at that warehouse!?!

{Richard} Look sweetheart I can't go into all the details. Because you already know. The less you know, the better off you and I would be.

{Patricia} Now you look Richard! The other day when I was coming home from the market. Two Detectives approached me. Asking me all kinds of questions about you, and Paul. And the rest of his crew.

{Richard} Oh really!?! What was their names?

{Patricia} Detectives Holman and Schultz. They said that, you are more important to their investigation dealing with Paul Meadows. Saying you know, everything that's been happening with Paul's operations. Especially that Damn warehouse!

{Richard} Well there's nothing that I can be able to help them with any investigation about Paul. So, they were harassing you to get to me!?!

{Patricia} Richard we don't have time for this nonsense! You; Paul, and his Merry Crew is going to get us either locked up or killed one! So, I don't know what you guys are up to, but I refuse to live life on the edge like that again. First when you away at war. Now with Paul again!?! What? The war life wasn't enough!?! Damn!

{Richard} Babe now look! We are not at war anymore . . . That life is over! The Meadows is on a new page. We're about changing lives.

{Patricia} Sure you are, but for the better or the worst?

Walking the Invisible Line
Shake; Rattle; and Roll

{As the crew approaches Baltimore, MD. Kym notifies Montego of their arrival.}

{Kym} Hello Montego, this is Kym, we should be arriving in about an hour.

{Porshia} Yeah, the sooner we can handle these Southsiderz . . . The sooner we can get back home!

{George} Yep! And get the Hell out of Romper room part of town! Where the heck we got to get these Southsiderz at . . . Sesame Street!?!

{Rachel} Yeah! I can see the crew now! Big Bird; Oscar The Grouch; Cookie Monster; Bert and Ernie; and oh yes, don't forget about Kermit de Frog! Yep! A real bad ass crew huh!?!

{Kym} Okay crew remember . . . It's not as easy as you think, it's going to be.

{Porshia} Well why the Hell not!?!

{Kym} Because First off, their young. Second; we need to get all of them damn near in one setting, or the whole plan would be in vain!

{Rachel} She's right y'all! The Southsiderz are a bunch of local hard heads that don't want to listen to nobody! They need to learn the lesson all in together now!

{George} Well make they're asses like the group Onyx and Slam! Duh duh duh! Duh duh duh! Let the boys, be boys! Slam!! Their Damn Heads All in Together Now!

{The crew laughs out loud and say.} SLAM!

{The crew meets up with Montego. For the shakedown instructions for the Southsiderz}

{Montego} Hello Meadows Crew. Unfortunately, we must meet on these unnecessary situations.

{Rachel} Very unnecessary situations!

{George} Well . . . Where they at?

{Montego} Well I hope you guys don't think it's going to be easy like Sunday Morning, because it's not! They're not going to come up to you and say Hey! Here we are!?! No, I don't think so!

{Kym} So, what's the best way to catch a rat!?! With cheese of course.

{George} So, what's for bait?

{Kym} Cash Rules Everything Around Me, Cream! Get that money! Alright Montego, set'em up!

{Montego calls the Southsiderz to an old warehouse on the east side of town.}

{George} I guess this is The Southsiderz coming in now.

{Montego} Yes, it's them. Right on schedule. Welcome Southsiderz! We have an offer for you guys. Since it's about 15 of you all. $30 Thousand, and you guys can give up the southside life. You guys can start a business. I can walk you through it. So, you would be very profitable!

{Max} Are you kidding me!?! We can make that in half a week or greater. Why should we give up something for a little of nothing!?!

{Porshia} Simple, because you guys want to live! That's why, any further questions?

{Max} The Southsiderz and myself say, no way are we . . . giving up anything! Now as far as I can see, this meeting is adjourned! Bye! Bye! Bitches!!

CHAPTER
9

RESPECT OUR TERRITORIES

No Time for Kiddie Games

{Montego} Well Max, don't say that I didn't try to help you guys out, but now you're on your own! Alright Meadows Crew, do what you came to do!

{George takes down Max, and the ladies pulls out their guns!}

{Kym} Alright! Nobody moves; nobody gets hurt! Now I believe that Montego gave you guys a fair price. We didn't come to talk, nor negotiate. We came to represent.

{Max} Hoe! I don't care what you came to say or do. Like I said . . .

{Just then George punches Max in the mouth!}

{George} Shut the hell up! Don't speak until we give you permission too! I see why we had to come! You guys really think this a game!?! Well it's not! The Meadows Crew owns warehouses all over the south side of Baltimore, and you guys are on our property!

{Max} I don't see The Meadows Crew name tatted on the Southside walls of Baltimore! So, who the Hell is y'all!?!

{Just then, Porshia puts her gun to Max's temple!}

{Porshia} Like the man just said, we're not here to discuss nothing with any of you! Respect our territories! Which is all of Baltimore's Southside! So, before I let my friend do the talking. You better shut up!

{Kym} Yes! Now the only way we'll let you, and your friends walk out of here. You guys listen, and I mean you better listen up! Southsiderz your services are no longer needed. So, take the offer that Montego given, and get the hell out of here!

{Max} What of crap is that!?! The Southsiderz is not giving up anything!

{George} Well alright! Phase 2!

{The Meadows dove into the Southsiderz! George pounding away at Max! Kym leaps at one of the ladies of the Southsiderz, and Porshia take shots at their crew.}

{Rachel} Kym! Lookout behind you!

{Kym turns around and punches one of the Southsiderz out cold! George takes down two more of their rivals.}

{Montego} Now you Southsiderz listen to me! The ones that's able to leave. Gather your friends and your losses. And get the hell up out of here! Now the deal is off, and I'm not going to repeat myself! Now get the Hell out of here!

{The Southsiderz gathered up the rest of their members and left the premises.}

{Rachel} I could not believe those damn Southsiderz! And that Max character! Boy oh boy! He couldn't keep his mouth shut!

{George} Until I shut it up for him, but you know how we do! Got to give them a helping hand; by shutting their mouths up for them. Like a steel gate over a store front, kaboom!

{Kym} Ha-ha! Yep! Just shut them down, or shall I say Shoot them down!

{Porshia} Yep, that too!

{The crew laughs}

{Meanwhile back at the warehouse. Paul talks with Samantha and Lavis.}

{Paul} Samantha! What happened to you, and Lavis for trip to Baltimore? I really needed all hands-on deck with that trip!

{Samantha} Paul if we knew that you needed us as well. We would've gone also.

{Lavis} Besides, we heard that not all the crew was needed on that trip. Because some us was needed to go and check out what's going on in Georgia!

WATCH YOUR STEP, AND TREAD LIGHTLY

{Paul} Lavis, I still need my crew in place for anything! Never know what might transpire! As a matter of fact, you guys have been M.I.A for some time now! Is there some love affair going on with you two?

{Samantha} Now Paul! Our business, is our business! You don't have to worry about that!

{Lavis} Most definitely our business!

{Paul} Look I'm not trying to intrude, or pry in y'all business; but that's risky business.

{Lavis} Look Paul, how is that risky?

{Paul} Because it can interfere with your better judgement dealing with operations. Not to mention, also dangerous in battle! Now I don't have anything against the unity between you two, but just be careful, alright!?!

{Samantha} We will Paul, we will!

{Lavis} For sure we will!

{Paul} Heaven forbid . . . If anything happens to one of you. The other will be out of commission.

{Samantha and Lavis answer simultaneous.} No! we won't!

{Paul} Alright then!

{Just then Paul's phone rings, and it's Montego!}

{Montego} Hey Paul! I have Good news, and Bad news.

{Paul} Give me the Good news first.

{Montego} Well the situation has been handled as far as The Southsiderz are in concern!

{Paul} And what's the Bad news?

{Montego} Well we have a bit of a mess to clean up.

{Paul shakes his head in disappointment.}

{Paul} Didn't I tell you guys Just a shakedown, not a permanent takedown!?! We don't need that kind of heat right now! So, what happened?

{Montego} Well Max, the head of The Southsiderz. Kept running off at the mouth. So, they shut it for him! Not permanently, but for a good while. Hell! With a mouth like that, it'll be running again!

{Paul} Damn! Why couldn't he just shut the Hell up!

{Just then Richard shows up at the door.}

{Richard} Hey Paul! What's going on in Baltimore? Oh, Hey Lavis; Samantha; what's good with you guys!?!

{Paul} Well I'm on the phone with Montego now! Finding out all the details. Uh, Montego. Put Kym on the phone.

{Kym} Yes Paul!?!

{Paul} Ok Kym what happened? Any causalities?

{Kym} Not now, but anything can change in a matter of time

{George} Tell Paul, we had to handle our business, and shut them up!

{Paul} Kym! Are any of our people hurt?

{Kym} Now you know better than that Paul!

{Meanwhile back in Baltimore . . . The Southsiderz are plotting revenge against the Meadows Crew.}

{Max} Yo, Tony! What's going on bro!?!

{Tony} Yeah bro I heard about some out of towners coming around here. Acting like; they own shit!

{Max} Yeah, but they going to pay for that! They go by the name of Meadows Crew.

{Tony} Where are they from!?!

{Max} I don't know but find out for me! Then we're going to handle them fools!

{Mitchell} Yeah cuz, we got you! We going to find them, then it's time for a 187!

{The Southsiderz replied} Hell yeah!

You Don't Want No Problems

{Richard} Paul! Now look, things are getting more out of hand. I just got word that the Detectives are regrouping and recruiting new officers on their squad. To further investigate our crew, and our operations.

{Paul} Well Richard, all we got to do is handle our business. Far as they are in concern, they're trying to earn stars and stripes!

{Samantha} We got to get things tight and right Paul! I'm starting to feel loose ends.

{Lavis} Yeah! As a matter of fact! Where Brandon at? I haven't seen nor heard from him. In a couple days now!

{Paul} Ok sense everybody becoming unraveled about the whole thing. We need to have a meeting about the police. Before they return with reinforcements. I'm waiting for the others to return. It's best that everybody knows at the same time.

{Kym} Alright Montego! Any more problems out of them Southsiderz, just let me know!

{Montego} There shouldn't be any more problems! Do you think!?!

{George} I think not, but who knows with them.

{Porshia} Well Damn! Max and five others took an ambulance ride. The others ran off. Humph! Some gangsters huh!?!

{Kym} Well we're on our way back home.

{Rachel} That Max got a lot of mouth! Damn near had the gun in his mouth, and still shooting off at the lips!

{Paul} Cats like that; learn their lessons the hard way.

{George} You know what Paul!?! Not only, the Southsiderz learn a lesson the hard way. The detectives will too, learn the hard way about The Meadows Crew!

{While Paul waits for his crew return, DT's Holman and Schultz are strategizing a plan of operation.}

{DT Holman} Hey Captain Harris, I really can use a team to help take down these drug lords on the Northern part of Nashville.

{Captain Harris} You guys don't quit do you!?! Do you have any idea on what this will cost the department!?!

{DT Holman} No I don't Captain! But I have a great intuition that you're going to tell me, aren't you!?!

{Captain Harris} You bet your ass I am! To have a team like that; there's protocol that we must abide by.

{DT Holman} Captain . . . I'm really starting to believe that we're letting the drug lords slide by, or shall I say Kingpins!

{DT Schultz} Aye, Detective Holman!

{DT Holman} What is it Schultz!?!

{DT Schultz} We got a lead on that Missing Persons Case.

{DT Holman} What Missing Person are you referring about?

{DT Schultz} Daniel's case. There's a gentleman that saw Mr. Daniels the night he went missing.

{DT Holman} Alright Captain, now what you got to say about this one?

{Captain Harris} Just because you may have a lead on the Daniels case. It doesn't mean that everything is going to fall into place. It's a very high-profile type of case. So, you better look; before you leap!

Detect the New Developments

{DT Holman} Ok Schultz, you got the lead; now we got something to go by!

{Captain Harris} Holman! Where you guys think you're going!?!

{DT Holman} Captain! Detective Schultz and I are going to follow up on this lead. This could possibly bring out the truth; about what happen to Mr. Daniels. And possibly the link to put Paul Meadows and his crew away.

{DT Schultz} Now the lead we're following, here's a picture. His name is Jason, and the best of it all; get this! He works for Ms. Kym Lei.

{DT Holman} Ah-ha! Well it seems to me that; we have a person of interest here!

{DT Schultz} You got it Holman! The only thing about it is . . . Getting Jason to talk.

{DT Holman} Well it all depends on the approach. Even if we got to send in a trusting decoy. Someone they can begin to trust!

{DT Schultz} Sounds very deceptive, but cunning enough to work on our behalf. But who's going to be our Go Getter Goose!?! Without becoming a Dead Damn Duck!

{DT Holman} Let me worry about the goose! Right now, we got a lead to investigate.

{Captain Harris} Detective Holman! You better know what you're doing! You and Schultz . . . Because if you don't and mess up; this will be on y'all heads! Understand!

{Holman slams the office door; without a reply!}

{Meanwhile back at the warehouse. Jason calls Kym; to take the rest of the day off.}

{Jason} Hello Kym, this is Jason.

{Kym} Hey Jason what's up!?!

{Jason} Look; today is a slow day Kym. So, I might be leaving early today.

{Kym} Not so Jay! I need you to stay at the warehouse. To keep an eye on production. Also, to make sure that the new line of fabrics, are moving like clockwork!

{Jason} Kym, I'm quite sure the crew can handle the fabrics. I would like to take an early leave today! I just have an uneasy feeling about today, and the pit; never lies!

{Kym} Look Jason! Don't leave the warehouse, for no apparent reason!

{Jason} Kym, just take my word for it! It will not be profitable for me to stay here.

{Kym} Jason, make like one songs from Jodeci, and just Stay!

{Jason} Well ok! Then you can also, make like one of their songs, and Come and Talk to Me! Pretty baby . . .

{Kym} Oh Jason I didn't know you cared. In that case; I'll be there shortly.

{Jason} Now that's more like it! I'm always here, and she's always in the fields. Hell, just last week she went to Baltimore! Damn, can I get a break!?! Like a kit Kat, or like Nell Carter used to say, Give Me A Break!

{At this time Kym leaves to meet Jason at the warehouse.}

EXPECT THE UNEXPECTED

{Brandon shows up at Paul's office.}

{Richard} Damn Brandon; where the hell, have you been!?!

{Brandon} I've been taking care of my meat markets. Exclusively the one in Chattanooga! I must keep my business afloat. So, what's been going on!?!

{Paul} Well you missed the action in Baltimore, MD. Kym and the ladies went with George. To meet Montego. So, they could handle a problem; we were having on the Southside of Baltimore.

{Brandon} What problem was that!?!

{Paul} The Southsiderz! A group of young wannabees that thought they was going to take over, but not so!

{Richard} Well I missed all the fun too huh!?! Not fair!

{Paul} Nope! I had you to go to Georgia, to make sure everything is going like it supposed to down there. Make no mistake! Soo I'm going to have guys going various locations.

{Lavis} What you mean by that Paul?

{Paul} As you know, we have really expanded across different regions, and so far, we locked down eight states. Now I'm looking forward to Michigan; Texas; Florida; and the Carolinas.

{Samantha} Damn Paul! What you trying to do? A National Takeover!?!

{Paul} Hell yeah! That's the goal. I thought you knew!?! Weren't you paying attention at the very first meeting? Don't act like you forgot!

{Samantha} Wow! Through all the excitement I must have forgotten all about it.

{Paul} Well ok then, you just been reminded of the original plan! Are you back to reality!?!

{Samantha} Yeah Paul, we're focused again.

{Samantha says sarcastically. Meanwhile Kym meets Jason at the warehouse.}

{Kym} Alright Jason! Now why would I have come to leave an important meeting? With Paul, of people! So, I can come and see what's going on here?

{Jason} Well Kym It's like this. You always out in the field, and I'm always here. Hell, don't you think that I need a break too from time to time. Nell Carter said it best, Give Me A Break!

{Kym} Well Jason, what kind of break are you looking for?

{Jason} I need a Y.O.U. break! A leave from here and take a break! In your world!

{Kym} Oh I see! So, where you want to go? Your break can start, right now!

{Jason} I know this lovely restaurant on the North side of Nashville.

{Kym} Well then, what are we waiting for? Let's go!

{Kym phone rings, and it's Paul.}

{Paul} Kym are you close by?

{Kym} No, I'm not Paul! I'm at the warehouse getting ready for my outing. I will call you back in few hours.

{Paul} Ok. But don't be too long!

{Kym} I won't Paul!

CHAPTER 10

Taking Out the Middle Man

Time for Elimination!

{Montego contacts Paul for a meeting; about eliminating the middle man.}

{Paul} What's going on Montego!?!

{Montego} Paul, me and you need to have a talk.

{Paul} Ok . . . About what?

{Montego} No! Not over the phone! I'm coming to Nashville tomorrow. So, I will call you when I get there.

{Paul} Alright Montego. See you tomorrow.

{The next day, Montego arrives at Paul's office.}

{Paul} What's good Montego? Now what did you want to discuss with me; that was so important. That we couldn't discuss over the phone!

{Montego} Well Paul . . . This what I've been thinking about for quite some time now.

{Paul} Well, what is it!?!

{Montego} Paul, are you satisfied with the product services from our contact?

{Paul} What!?! I hope you not saying; what I think you're trying say! Montego! Are you talking about . . . Eliminating the Middle Man!?!

{Montego} Yeah, that's what I'm talking about. What I'm saying is, we can get more accomplished by doing so. Instead of paying the middle man. Remember! We have teams that we need to accommodate financially.

{Paul} Yeah; I hear you Montego, but I don't know if that's the right move at this point and time. Montego I really got to think about this.

{Meanwhile Samantha and Lavis talks about upcoming events.}

{Samantha} Lavis! What day are we going to Tampa Bay?

{Lavis} Thursday afternoon at 3pm. We're going to take the jet. You know Shawn at the airport. He's our pilot.

{Samantha} Yes, but this time we are going for a little bit of business; and a whole lot of pleasure.

{Lavis} Yes! To seek our new territories and take some sporadic time for ourselves. Two whole days!

{Samantha} Oh I can't wait to we get there!

{Even though The Meadows Crew are handling their business. Detectives Holman and Schultz are on their own mission.}

{DT Holman} Look we need to get to the location; where we can catch up with Jason. He's the one that can help us crack down on The Meadows Crew!

{DT Schultz} We'll go to the warehouse, and you know what the Commissioner said about us being at their warehouse! Do you want to go through that again Holman!?!

{DT Holman} No Schultz, not this time! We have a lead that we must follow up and questioned. Hopefully we can make him an offer that he can't refuse.

{DT Schultz} Yeah, but first! Catching up with him is the tedious part. Then see if we can convince Jason to tell us what he knows about the Daniel's Disappearance.

THERE'S A SHIFTING IN THE AIR!

{Rachel} Richard, where's George? Haven't heard from him since the other day.

{Richard} Don't worry about George. He's taking care of business in Memphis. Then he got to go back to Georgia tomorrow. To make sure the guns are moving like clockwork.

{Rachel} Well ok, I got to make sure everything is moving according to plan. We don't have time for errors. How's Patricia doing?

{Richard} She's fine! Although she hasn't been feeling well lately.

{Rachel} What do you mean?

{Richard} She's been complaining about pain in her stomach. She needs to go to the doctor, to see what's going on.

{Rachel} I hope everything will be alright with her!

{Richard} Yeah me too. As a matter of fact; I'm going to make her an appointment ASAP!

{Rachel} Yes, I think you need to do that for her sake!

{The Detectives are on the move for the warehouse.}

{DT Holman} Well Schultz, back at the warehouse on a different stakeout this time.

{DT Schultz} Yelp! So, we're here to catch up with Jason. Maybe he can give us some information about the Daniel's Disappearance.

{Meanwhile Kym and Jason are on their way out from the warehouse.}

{DT Schultz} Look Holman, there's Jason; and will you look at here . . . Ms. Kym Lei is with him also.

{DT Holman} Well, well, well! Let's go and have a talk with them shall we!?!

{DT Schultz} Indeed we shall. Let's go!

{The Detectives exits the vehicle and approaches the two.}

{DT Holman} Well! Look at here Schultz! It's Ms. Kym and Jason. What do you know about huh!?!

{DT Schultz} Well I be damn . . . It's Kym and Jason; Jason and Kym Hi, and how you two doing on this fabulous day!?!

{Kym} We're doing just fine officers! On our way to brunch. I'm quite sure you guys don't want to tag along.

{Jason} Exactly right Kym! This is an A, and B Rendezvous, there's no room for C, and D!

{DT Holman} On contrary, we're not tagging along at all!

{Kym} Ha! I thought so!

{DT Holman} But, Jason isn't going to brunch neither! So, Jason will be coming with us down to the station. So, we can ask you some questions.

{Jason} No! Me and Ms. Kym are going to brunch this afternoon. So, the answer is No! Flat-foot 1 and 2!

{DT Schultz} Oh you're so wrong Mr. Jason! Now you can either come with us willingly, or unwillingly by placing you under arrest!

{DT Holman} Huh! The choice is yours!

OMG! What A Disturbance!

{Taking Jason down to the station; surely wasn't a walk in the park!}

{Jason} Alright you guys! I agreed to come down here. So, now what!?!

{DT Holman} Well Jason! I'm going to get right to the point! What do you know about the disappearance of Mr. Daniels?

{DT Schultz} Yes, we have reason to believe that he's been murdered!

{Jason} Now how do you go, from a Missing Persons Case to a Homicide Case! So, now you guys believe; he was murdered!

{DT Holman} Starting to look that way! Disappeared without a trace!?! No signs; no track records of relocations . . . No nothing! Just gone, poof! Evaporated into thin air!

{Jason} Well I don't know what happened to Mr. Daniels!

{DT Schultz} Maybe not, but you do know who he was with! Going to see, the night he went missing.

{Jason} I can assure you guys; that I have no idea who he with the night in question! Besides Daniels never told us anything.

{DT Holman} I bet the differ! Now Jason. You better start telling us the truth, or you're going to do some time.

{Jason} Time! Time for what!?!

{DT Schultz} For conspiracy in connection with the disappearance and possibly murder of Mr. Daniels. Now you can rest assure on this! If Mr. Daniels turns up dead. Believe me when I tell you that; you're going down as number 1 suspect!

{Jason} Are you guys through? If so, can I go now!?!

{DT Holman} No! Not till we say so! Get comfortable Jay! Looks like you're going to be here for a while!

{Samantha and Lavis boarding the plane for their trip.}

{Lavis} Well babe, we're ready to take flight to parlay! In good old Tampa Bay.

{Samantha} Yes! Two days to get away for a vacay!

{Shawn} Ok we're ready for take-off. We should be arriving about 6pm.

{After the discussion with Paul and Montego, Paul gets a call from Kym!}

{Paul} Hello Kym. How's everything going at the warehouse!?!

{Kym} Not so good! The two detectives just took Jason down to the station! They are trying to gather information up Daniel's Disappearance. They're really getting pushy with this case.

{Paul} What are their plans of operation?

{Kym} My guess is: Good cop; Bad cop!

{Paul} Find out his bail!

{Kym} Jason's not under arrest. But he's being held for questioning. To see what he knows.

{Paul} Kym! I hope he keeps his mouth shut.

{Kym} Me too Paul; Me too.

{Samantha} When we get there Lavis; to the hotel we go. Change our clothes, and then we go to the new uncharted territory. That we'll be supplying.

{Lavis} Ok so, it's the hotel, and then go look at the new location for services.

{Shawn} Alright guys! We're going to be landing momentarily!

{Lavis} Great! That didn't take long at all. Two hours tops, and thirty minutes was driving time.

{Samantha} Well babe, we're here!

Do What You Got to Do!

{Jason still being detained at the police station!}

{DT Holman} Ok Jason look, we been here going back and forth with these allegations.

{Jason} We can eliminate all the back and forth crap by letting me go! I have nothing more to say to you guys without my lawyer being present.

{DT Holman} Ok who's your lawyer?

{Jason} Well I need to make a call, and then I'll let you know who's my lawyer!

{They let Jason makes his call, but best believe it's to Paul!}

{Jason} Hello Paul!?! It's Jason.

{Paul} Yes Jason. Kym just informed me that you're being detained at the police station.

{Jason} Yes! So, I was wondering if you can contact your lawyer for me. To get me out of this mess!

{Paul} Don't worry about a thing Jason! I'll have my lawyers there ASAP! I'm calling them now! Kym you go down to the station, and comfort Jason till my lawyers get there. And keep me posted!

{Kym} No problem; I'm on my way. Either way he has nothing to worry about. Jason don't know what happened. Jason don't even have a clue about that night.

{Paul} Good! Now you see why I emphasized from the very first meeting. Not to let everyone in the business. Never let your right hand know; what the left one is doing! The less people know; the further we'll go!

{Kym} I know that's right! Loose lips sink ships!

{Paul} And . . . Snitches get stitches too!

{They both laughed!}

{Paul contacts his lawyers. To come and resolve the situation that Jason is in!}

{Paul} Hello . . . Is this The Manning Law Firm!?!

{Secretary} Yes, it is The Manning Law Firm; And whom am I speaking with?

{Paul} Hello, my name is Paul Meadows. I am one Joseph and Tasha Manning's clients. I would like to speak with either one of them.

{Secretary} Yes Mr. Meadows, I can transfer you to Mr. Manning's phone line. Just hold while I transfer you're call Sir . . .

{Paul} Certainly my dear and thank you for time madam.

{Secretary} No problem, and your welcome Mr. Meadows.

{Joseph} Hello Joseph Manning, how may I help you!?!

{Paul} Well Joe! How you been? It's Paul!

{Joseph} Paul Meadows?

{Paul} Yes. It's been a long time Joe. How's your wife doing?

{Joseph} She's been great. No complaints here. So, Paul what's up!?!

{Paul} Well it looks like I'm going to need you and your wife's services. You see there's a little bit of mistaken identity in a missing persons case. That two Detectives are trying to pin on me, but they have No case!

{Joseph} Well, well; well! So, by what I'm hearing. You need our Bulldogging Services!

{Paul} Yes! I need you two Bulldogs to handle this situation we have here.

{Joseph} Alright Paul! How soon, do you need us?

{Paul} Hell, how soon can you get here?

{Joseph} 45 minutes tops!

{Paul} Alright Joe . . . See you when get here.

New Leverage for the Law!

{Kym arrives at the police station.}

{Jason} Hey Kym! What you doing here? These fools going to have to let me go! They don't have nothing on me!

{Kym} Of course not. I don't understand why they came messing with you in the first place! Evidently, they had that in mind. To come take you down for questioning.

{Jason} Yeah well, but what Paul got in mind for this situation at hand?

{Kym} In fact he does, his lawyers are going to be handling the situation for us! Which reminds me I got to call Paul for the updates.

{Samantha and Lavis at the Hotel. Changing for the evening.}

{Lavis} Okay babe; we got an area to check out. For new services. Got to make it snow in the south!

{Samantha} Yeah babe! It's hot down here! It can really use some cooling off! Shit, and I'm not talking about February either!

{Lavis} So, where we going to babe? North end, or the South end of Tampa Bay!?!

{Samantha} We're going to the North end. To meet a Realtor by the name of Charles.

{Lavis} Charles! Who's that!?!

{Samantha} Well he knows Paul. He's another one of Paul's connections through the real estate business.

{Lavis} So, I guess it's safe to say that; Paul's got Charles in Charge!

{Samantha} I'm going to in contact with Paul and see what time we supposed to meet this guy!

{Meanwhile Richard talks to Patricia, about going to the doctor's.}

{Richard} Look honey, I think it'll be a great idea for you to see the doctor.

{Patricia} Come on Richard. There's nothing wrong with me. I just had some pain in my stomach, but I'm okay babe.

{Richard} You been having that pain in your tummy for some time now. Approximately two to three weeks.

{Patricia} Okay babe! Well go to the doctor's office.

{Richard} Good! I'll make you an appointment ASAP!

{With no time to waste Richard calls to make an appointment for his wife.}

{Secretary} Hello Dr. Reeves office. How may I help you?

{Richard} Hello my name Richard Miles. I'm calling to make an appointment for my wife Patricia.

{Secretary} Yes, I can surely help you with that. Now what's troubling her?

{Richard} Well she's been having pains in her stomach for almost a month. Three weeks to be exact.

{Secretary} Wow! That's a long time to be dealing with stomach pains! Can you guys get in here tomorrow at 10am?

{Richard} We'll be there in the morning!

{Secretary} Good, we'll see you guys then!

{Richard} Ok, thank you so much for all your help.

{Secretary} No problem Mr. Miles! Glad to be a help for Mrs. Miles! See you tomorrow!

CHAPTER
11

NEW METHOD; NEW CHALLENGES

An Unfortunate
Thing Happened

{Samantha and Lavis leaves the hotel. To meet Charles at his warehouse.}

{Lavis} Now shouldn't Paul be contacting us about meeting this guy? I don't have a good feeling about this. Something just don't set right with me about this meeting here.

{Samantha} Oh Lavis stop worry! We're going to go and meet with Charles, and then we're off for our sporadic vacation.

{Lavis} Well I guess you're right. I'll call Paul and see if he contacted Charles and got the address.

{Lavis calls Paul to see if he got the information about the meet.}

{Paul} Hello Lavis, and how are things going in the Tampa Bay area.

{Lavis} So far so good; just wondered if you got in contact with Charles. So, we know where to go to meet him!?!

{Paul} Why yes, I did! The address is 3390 Faulkner Lane. He's looking forward to seeing you guys around 6pm.

{Lavis} Okay we'll be ready to go meet him then. By the way have you heard anything from Brandon or George!?!

{Paul} Not since last week. Brandon been focusing on the meat markets. He has three to maintain. The one in Memphis, and Chattanooga, and Nashville. And as for George . . . He's making sure the guns are moving like they supposed to!

{Lavis} Wow! You got things moving like clockwork huh!?!

{Samantha} Come now babe! We got to go so we can meet Charles. You have the address?

{Lavis} Yes babe! Alright Paul we're on our way! Ok babe let's go!

{George catches up with Brandon in Memphis, at the meat market.}

{George} Hey Brandon! What's going on man!?! Damn we don't hardly hear from you anymore! What!?! You don't have love for us no more?

{Brandon} Ha-ha! Very funny. No, it's not that! I'm running three meat markets, and I must make sure everything is running like it's suppose to. But if, or whenever you guys need me. Just holla, and I'll be there!

{George} Yeah, I hear you bro! So, I got to give you the heads up for the week.

{Brandon} What's going on for next week!?!

{George} We have another shipment coming in next Thursday. As a matter of fact. Samantha and Lavis are checking out the area in Tampa Bay; right now, as we speak.

{Brandon} Look I got to take out these cases of chicken to the storage out back. Could you help me with these cases?

{George} Sure dude, lead the way.

{Just as they we're walking out the door, a dark van drives along side the pathway of the building.}

{George} Hey Brandon . . . Do you know these guys; that just pulled up in a dark van?

{Brandon} No I don't. Hey uh, may I help you?

{Strangers from the Van} Yeah . . . You can help us.

{Just then the strangers pulled out guns on Brandon and George!}

{Stranger 1} Drop the damn food and put your hands up! Turn and face the wall!

{George} It's obvious you guys don't know who you're dealing with!

{Stranger 2} Shut the hell up man! No! You didn't know who the hell, you were messing with!

{Brandon} George! What the hell is he talking about? He's talking like he knows you, or something!

{Stranger 1} Oh we know him, and his bitches!

{George} Say what!?! Man, what the Hell are you talking . . .

{Interrupting George's talk; the strangers shoots George and Brandon in their backs!}

{Stranger 1} Yeah, you and your crew! That came to Baltimore. Let this be a lesson to you. Nobody messes with The Southsiderz and get away with it! Oh, and FYI! I'm Tony Max's cousin.

{Stranger 2} I'm Mitchell, Max's brother. You guys get comfy in your own blood.

All Hell's Breaking Loose!

{Samantha} Well Lavis, we should be arriving at the warehouse momentarily. So, when we meet with Charles. He's going to show us the layout, and the areas.

{Lavis} I don't know, but I think Paul is moving to fast! He needs to Slow it down!

As we all know; you can't tell Paul nothing!

{Samantha} Stop worrying babe! Paul knows what he's doing.

{Lavis} Humph! I hope you're right. Has anybody heard from George or Brandon? Hell, I hope their ok.

{Samantha} Yeah, me too! We haven't heard anything from those two in a few days.

{Lavis} Well we're here! Let's go meet Charles. You got your heat on you?

{Samantha} Damn straight I'm strapped! What about you?

{Lavis} Like an American Express Card, never leave home without it! Momma didn't raise no fool! And didn't Scar from The Lion King said, "Be Prepared!" Ok, here we go.

{Charles} Hello! Lavis and Samantha, I presume!?!

{Lavis} You presume correctly.

{Charles} Well this is our humble abode, our warehouse. Nothing fancy, but it's in an excellent location.

{Samantha} That it is Charles! So, where are the special compartments? Or shall I say secret

{Charles} Well in that case, follow me.

{Kym} What are we going to do Jason? Those DT's are not going to stop harassing about Daniel's Disappearance.

{Jason} I don't know what to do, but I'm waiting for the Lawyers to come through.

{Kym} Oh my GOD! I can't wait neither!

{At this time; Paul receives a call from the first responders team!}

{EMS 1} Hello, this is EMS 1! I'm calling you Sir; because . . . Two gentlemen that you might know has been shot!

{Paul} Shot!

{EMS 1} Yes sir shot! In the alleyway of a meat market in Memphis!

{Paul} Who are the gentlemen that you are referring about!?!

{EMS 1} Well the First one his name is George Matthews, and the second ones name is Brandon Wiley. I believe he owns this meat market, and two others as well.

{Paul} Well my name is Paul Meadows, and yes; they work for me! How are they!?! I really hope they're not seriously injured!

{EMS 1} Well we're transporting them to the hospital now! They we're both shot in the back. I'm praying that they'll pull through.

{Paul} Yes! I'm on the way to the hospital! And I want a full report on their conditions when I get there . . . Kalpesh!

{EMS 1} Well the doctors are going to give you that information. So, the sooner you get here the better!

{Paul} Oh yes! I'm coming, but best believe me, I'm bringing reinforcements with me. Which means I will not be alone!

A Major Gathering at the Vanderbilt

{Now that Paul found out the news about George and Brandon. It's time to call up the crew.}

{Paul} Hey Kym, how are you? This is Paul, look I just got a call from the EMS out in Memphis. Stating that George and Brandon were shot!

{Kym} What!?!

{Paul} Yes! It caught me off guard as well. So, I want you to call up the ladies, and I will call Richard and Lavis. Samantha is with him now in Tampa Bay.

{Kym} Oh my GOD! Ok I'll get on the horn right away! Samantha and Lavis are going to be pissed off about this!

{Paul} Yes, they are! But I need everyone to get together as soon as possible. So, we can get to the hospital ASAP!

{Kym} Ok, but which one are they're in!?!

{Paul} They were transported to the Vanderbilt in Nashville. They will be in the best of care there.

{Kym} Alright! I'm going to call them now; bye Paul!

{Paul and Kym commenced on calling the crew!}

{Porshia} Now who's calling me? Hello.

{Kym} Hey Porshia how are you doing? This is Kym.

{Porshia} Oh hey girl, what's going on? I thought you were one of those pesky callers! 1 900; 1 800; crazy ass numbers!

{Kym} Girl! No time for games, this is not a social call.

{Porshia} Well Damn Kym! What's up?

{Somehow, Kym got to soften the blow. To be able to tell Porshia what's really going on!}

{Kym} Well the crew must meet Paul at the Vanderbilt Hospital in Nashville!

{Porshia} Wait! wait; wait; wait! Hold up . . . What happened, and where he at again!?!

{Kym} He's at the Vanderbilt, we got to go see George and Brandon! They got shot a little while ago.

{Porshia} Oh my GOD!! Ok I'm going to call Rachel and Samantha!

{Kym} Paul already called Lavis, and Sam was with him. So, by now she knows!

{Meanwhile Richard and Patricia are at the Vanderbilt.}

{Richard} Alright Doc! What did the test results show? Since my wife been through various tests. Enough of the waiting and anticipating.

{Doctor} Well the results are in, but unfortunately there's a significant sign of cancer in the small intestine.

{Patricia} What! How can this be? Are you sure Doctor!?! I mean the test can be wrong!

{Richard} No! This cannot be so, Doc! What can be done to prevent cancer from spreading anywhere else!?!

{Doctor} Well there's chemo, but we have got to make sure she can be able to handle the procedure.

{Patricia} Yes Doctor, whatever needs to be done . . . Let's get it started!

{Richard} Damn straight! I not losing my wife over no cancer! So, do what you got to do Doc! Money is no object, and that's final!

THE VANDERBILT GATHERING

{The crew meet up at Vanderbilt Hospital, in hopes to find out what happened.}

{Paul} Hello Kym!

{Kym} Hey Paul. Rachel and Porshia should be here soon. Did you contact Lavis and Samantha?

{Paul} Yes! There on their way back.

{Kym} I know they hated to cut their trip short!

{Paul} Yes, I know but the family is in crisis right now, and we got to find out. What really happened to our guys!

{Kym} Paul! You don't suspect that, they got shot because; of what happened in Baltimore, MD.

{Paul} I don't know Kym, but we're going to find out. One way, or another. So, what's going with Jason?

{Kym} The lawyers you sent are handling the case. So, he has nothing to worry about.

{Just then Rachel and Porshia, entered in the lobby.}

{Porshia} Hey guys we're here now! How's George and Brandon doing?

{Paul} I don't know! We haven't been upstairs yet. I've been trying to contact Richard, but no such luck.

{Rachel} Well don't we need to go upstairs? So, we can find out what's going on?

{Paul} I guess so crew. We got to go to the 3rd floor to ICU.

{The crew goes to ICU to check on George and Brandon, but just to find out that Richard and Patricia are there also.}

{Richard} Paul! Kym; Rachel; Porshia . . . What are you guys doing here!?!

{Paul} Got Damn man! I've been calling you Rich! Blowing up your phone bro! Where you been man?

{Richard} Been here with my wife! I couldn't answer no phone calls, because of the low reception in this part of the hospital. Besides what's going on?

{Paul} Well the reason I've been calling, is because our guys George and Brandon has been shot!

{Richard} What the Hell! Where were they when this happened?

{Paul} In Memphis! Outside of Brandon's Market place. The EMS called and told me they got shot in the back. Alongside the alleyway.

{Richard} Do Lavis and Samantha know about this?

{Paul} Yep! I called and told Lavis! So, how are you guys? Is Patricia ok?

{Patricia} Well the doctor said that in my small intestine. My tests show signs of cancer. So, they must act aggressively. For me to have a fair chance of survival.

{Rachel} Oh my GOD!

{Paul} Damn! Look you guys, if there's anything you guys need; just let me know! I don't give a damn what it is!

{Richard} Thanks Paul! Now let's go and find out about George and Brandon!

{Patricia} I hope they're going to be alright!?!

{Porshia} We're hoping and praying for the same thing!

{They all gathered together in a circle. For a moment of prayer.}

{Richard} Heavenly Father . . . We come to You; Humble as we know how . . .

Dear Father . . . Please! Bring our brothers back to us. Heal their bodies, Strengthen them now Father GOD! In JESUS Name! We pray! Amen! Amen! Amen!

{Patricia} That's right babe! HE's the One, and only one who can help them!

NEW STRATEGIC MOVES, IN THE ICU!

{Samantha and Lavis are on their way back. To meet the crew at the Vanderbilt Hospital.}

{Samantha} I just can't believe; that someone would just want to kill George and Brandon! It just doesn't make any sense! I mean like, why!?!

{Lavis} I don't know babe! Remember . . . George, and the other ladies just came back. Not to long ago from Baltimore. You know what we're dealing with . . . The Southsiderz!

{Samantha} Oh my GOD! You don't think that, they would have something to do with George and Brandon getting shot!?!

{Lavis} It's the only thing I can think of, and they'll be the ones with a motive. We got to get back to the airport. So, we can get to our jet. Where Shawn will meet us and take us home.

{Paul} Ok crew listen up! We going to find out the truth about what happened. I'm just that determined; to find the ones that are responsible for all this. Then make them wish, they were never born!

{Kym} No problem Paul! All we need is a name.

{Porshia} Uh huh! Make them pay dearly! When Lavis and Samantha supposed to be getting here?

{Paul} They should be arriving about two hours, or so it won't take them long! Remember, we have our own private jet.

{Samantha} Ok honey we're here! Now we must get to the hospital. Damn! Talk about the jet lagged feeling!

{Lavis} True babe! Shawn flew by turbo jet!

{Paul and his crew reaches the ICU floor, and yes . . . Their looking for answers!}

{Kym} Oh good there's the doctor! Hey Doc! We are friends of the two guys that were shot, In Memphis by the meat market.

{Doctor} Yes of course! Right now, the surgeon is operating on Brandon now. George is in ICU on a respirator machine.

{The crew gasped in disbelief!}

{Paul} Are they going to be alright doctor?

{Doctor} Well I'm going to be frank with you all. George is out of surgery, but not out of the woods, and we got to wait and pray for Brandon!

{Kym} Why!?! What's his disposition after the shooting?

{Doctor} Brandon was struck in the left lower lung. Which caused some internal bleeding. Possibly hemorrhaging as well. So, George is in and out of consciousness, but can barely speak. Brandon it's touch and go with him.

{Paul} If it's possible doctor; I need to speak with George!

{Doctor} Well I can go and check in on George. Wait here in the lobby. I'll be back to let you guys know what's going on.

{Paul} Thank you doctor. Kym do me a favor. We might have to go to the scene of the crime to be able to get some answers. So, I want to call the meat market in Memphis. Ask for the assistant manager that's working under Brandon. To find out what you can. Understood!

{Kym} I'm on it Paul!

CHAPTER
12

THE ELEMENT OF SURPRISE

Keep Hope Alive!

{Jason calls Kym, to let her know that he has been released.}

{Kym} Hello! Hi Jason! Where are you?

{Jason} I'm on my way home now. The Manning's got me released on the grounds for; lack of evidence. Besides, they don't want a law suit.

{Kym} Good! I'm glad you're out. We got enough on our plate as it is.

{Jason} What's wrong Kym?

{Kym} Well I told you that I had to meet with Paul and the crew. It's because George and Brandon got shot in Memphis. Outside of Brandon's market.

{Jason} Oh GOD! I'm willing to bet you, a hundred to one . . . It was those Southsiderz.

{Kym} The ones we had to battle it out over the south end of Baltimore?

{Jason} Yep!

{Kym} Well; how can you be so sure!?!

{Jason} I got that feeling that. Those local wannabees would do anything, just to build up their reputation!

{Kym} Okay babe! I'm going to investigate this for sure!

{Jason} Well you sure don't have far to look.

{Paul} Okay Doctor! What's the verdict?

{Doctor} Ok, George is awake, but mind you . . . He's heavily sedated currently. My guess is; that you can go in and see him for a few minutes.

{Rachel} Alright you guys! They only going to allow two at a time to see George.

{Kym} Me and Paul, will go in first so, we can find out what he knows.

{Meanwhile the Southsiderz celebrating they're meantime victory!}

{Max} What you say Southsiderz! We surely took out those fools for crossing us! Hey Mitchell, are you sure they dead!?!

{Mitchell} Hell we shot them down in the alleyway. Ain't nobody surviving that!

{Max} Well I really hope you guys took them out! Cause we don't need to see them no more!

{Tony} Yeah cuz! There's no way, those two will survive what we put on them! So, chill and relax.

{Samantha} Hey what's up everybody!?! What's the status on George and Brandon?

{Lavis} Yeah! Are they okay or what!?! Most importantly . . . Who's responsible for this?

{Porshia} We're going to find out who's behind all this! But we got to wait until George can tell us something.

{Samantha} You mean to tell me George, nor Brandon can tell us anything yet!?!

{Rachel} That's right. Hopefully he's aware enough to tell us something. Brandon on the other hand he's still in surgery. He's worst of the George.

{Porshia} They're both in ICU. George is on a breathing machine, and there's no telling what condition Brandon's in. When or if he makes it out of surgery. It's touch and go with him!

{Lavis} Oh Brandon's tuff as nails! He'll make it out alright! We got to remember, we fought in Afghanistan. We are Marines! If we were The A Team he would be B.A. Barrackas, and I pity the fool who messed with our guys!

Keep Your Guard Up

{Back at the station, DT Holman is putting together a squadron of his own.}

{DT Holman} Now that the department got its budget for the new appointed officers for my team. We can start cracking down on Paul, and his crew! We are going to nail him, and his crew!

{DT Shultz} How are we supposed to crack down on them. When the one lead we had fell through the cracks!

{DT Holman} Well you see Shultz. Now that the department has more money. Captain Harris can't company budget. So, now I can put a division together to help take down the Meadows Crew!

{DT Shultz} Ok so, who's the number 1 draft pick?

{DT Holman} Officer Cole. Military trained, also Marine Corp Veteran. Yeah! The Meadows Crew finally going to meet their match. When I'm finished getting my division together. It's going to be on, and popping!

{DT Shultz} Who's next?

{DT Holman} Officer Peele is next, on the division's menu. Another Marine Corp Vet. That's no joke!

{DT Shultz} Now I get it! To catch a Marine, you got to be a Marine! Takes one to know one huh!?!

{DT Holman} Exactly Shultz! Ok let's see who's next? Officers Holland; Williams; Hart; and Frye! We got to get these officers to the meeting room.

{DT Shultz} Alright Holman! We got the officers; now we need the strategy to plan and proceed. To go after Paul Meadows and his crew.

{The new recruited officers meeting.}

{DT Holman} Good morning officers. You guys probably wondering what this meeting is all about!?! It's about collaborating a new division. A division to take down a high classed notorious mob. They go by the name of The Meadows Crew.

{DT Shultz} Yes, but keep in mind; that the Meadows Crew ain't nothing to play around with! Their very tactical and specially trained. Military background and all.

{Officer Peele} Yeah, well so are we! With us you have two from the Marine Corp. Two from the Army, and two Navy Seals.

{Officer Williams} That's right! I'm a retired Navy Seal. My base is SWAT, but for now all I can say is. When you come up against us, you better know what you're doing!

{DT Holman} Huh, I heard that! Yeah Paul, keep ya' guard up. Cause we're coming for you, and your crew!

{Officer Hart} According to what I heard about Paul. He's quite the mastermind behind the crew. I wonder what he has been shipping in at their beloved docks.

{DT Holman} Well it ain't lumber that's for sure!

{DT Shultz} More like guns and drugs. Alongside with fabrics and school supplies. Trouble is we've been unsuccessful in catching them with the guns and drugs. To take them down.

{Officer Williams} When there's a will; there's a way!

{DT Shultz} A way for what Williams?

{DT Williams} To take down a Damn Kingpin!

THE WINDS DON'T BLOW WITH EASE.

{Richard} If it ain't one thing it's another all the time! Never a dull moment.

{Patricia} Oh come now Richard! You got to get a hold of yourself. It's best that we found out what's going on with me now. Verses finding out much later.

{Richard} I understand babe, but you got to understand where I'm coming from. Cause babe I love you! You're my heart; my love; my everything! I can't bare the thought of losing you.

{Patricia} Baby don't you worry! The doctor said, being that the cancer was detected early. They can eliminate the cancer cells before they start to spread.

{Richard} I know sweetheart; I know! I'm glad about the early detection, but why you!?!

{Patricia} Baby listen to me! We can't determine what GOD has in store for us! Only thing we can do, is do right by HIM, and everything is going to be alright.

{Richard} You're right babe! As usual your right.

{The doctor calls to inform Patricia about an upcoming appointment. To start the procedure.}

{Doctor} Ok Mrs. Miles, I'm scheduling you for a consultation meeting. About the upcoming procedures, and treatments. Don't you worry about a thing! We're going to take good care of you.

{Patricia} That's good to know. I am a bit nervous, but my husband is more of a wreck than I am.

{Doctor} Ha-ha! Tell him not to worry, because worrying makes the situation worst. So, rest assure that you Mrs. Miles. Are in the best of care.

{Back at the Vanderbilt Hospital, Paul is determined to get answers.}
{Paul} George!?!
{George replies, soft and vague.}

{George} Yeah . . . Paul, is that you?

{Paul} Yep! It's me, but most importantly . . . how are you feeling?

{George} Like a man that just got shot! Thank GOD, for morphine! Got me feeling high as a kite. Paul! How's Brandon doing is he ok!?!

{Paul} Well it's touch and go with him right now. I mean he's still in ICU. His left lung was struck by a bullet. He has a way to go before he's completely out the woods. Hopefully we'll hear something before nightfall.

{Samantha and Lavis has entered the room.}

{Lavis} Hey champ! How you feeling today?

{George} High as a kite. You see what they got me hooked up to!

{Samantha} Morphine! Oh yeah, you're feeling quite good right now.

{Paul} George! Did you see the who did this to you and Brandon?

{George} I surely remember them saying Southsiderz for life! One of them name is Mitchell, Max's brother and the other name was Tony Max's cousin.

{Paul} So, it was two of the Southsiderz who did this Huh!?!

{George} Yeah it was them. The dumb thing about it is. They told us their damn names!

{Paul} Alright Southsiderz! You wanted war, well dammit! Welcome to Hell! I promise you. You have no clue; of what we're capable of!

{George} What you going to do Paul?

{Paul} Tear some asses up! Cold featuring; The Southsiderz!

{George} Well damn! Have fun.

{Paul} Oh believe me . . . I will!

A Toast for the Takeout!

{The truth is out about George and Brandon's assailants. So, now it's time to take out the trash!}

{Paul} Look George you get your rest, and we'll take care of the rest!

{Samantha} Yeah! Don't you worry about a thing! The Meadows Crew got it all under control.

{Lavis} That's right! We'll take care of it George. We going to check on Brandon and see how he's doing.

{George} You guys go do that. I got to get some rest. The morphine has kicked in again. Look when I wake up, I'll ask the nurse about Brandon.

{Paul} Fair enough, we'll be back to check on you.

{Samantha} Yeah George! You get your rest, and we'll see you later.

{George} Yeah guys later!

{Lavis} So, now what Paul!?! It was two from The Southsiderz that shot George and Brandon!

{Kym} Them Southsiderz really want some heat, don't they?

{Paul} Whelp! They going to get; what they been looking for!

{Rachel} Yep! They just found it!

{Porshia} You all know; how the story goes. Time to take that ride . . . To the Southside of Baltimore!

{Paul} Well that's general idea, but there's going to plan in place for the Southsiderz!

{Everybody shouted simultaneously . . . Damn Straight!}

{As Paul contemplates a plan for the Southsiderz, Montego makes the phone call to arrange his own takeout order!}

{Montego} Hey Elm, this Montego. I need for you to meet me at my office. To discuss about the project, I want you to do for me. Can you meet me in an hour?

Excellent! I'll see you then.

{Paul} Now that everyone is here. I will say this briefly. Tony and Mitchell will be taking a trip. All expense paid vacation. That they can really relax and enjoy. A trip, they will not come back from.

{Samantha} Shall we arrange, The Dinner Flight; or shall it be Plan C?

{Paul} Group plan C it is. Porshia and Rachel, set it up. The sooner the better!

{Rachel} No problem! Set it up like hook; line, and sinker.

{Porshia} I'm ready to put the gun down their throats and squeeze slow! Kind of make their life flash before their eyes and then . . . Bang!

{Paul} I'll tell you when to spring everything into action. Hell, I want them to disappear without a trace. As a matter of fact!

{Lavis} What method Paul!?!

{Paul} Kym! I want them; clean as a whistle!

{Kym} How clean do you want them?

{Paul} I want them so clean . . . that they are clear, like water! In other words, liquidate they asses!

{Kym} Just make it a bath for them!

{Paul} Excellent choice Kym!

{The crew is in full agreement!}

No Delaying for Death

{A knock came at the door. Montego answers, and it's Elm!}

{Montego} Glad you can make it Elm! Come on in.

{Elm} Thank you. So, what you want to discuss about?

{Montego} What I want to talk to you about is that. Paul and myself are willing to have the middle man eliminated!

{Elm} So, this is where I come in at?

{Montego} Yes! We need your sniper skills to take out Malachi! He's the key connection for our supplies.

{Elm} Well, if you take out Malachi, then who's going to be the contact person for the supplies, and shipment?

{Montego} We are, Paul and myself can handle all the incoming. We might as well! Malachi been making too many mistakes.

{Elm} Alright now! Remember once the bomb is set, there's no turning back! Are you sure this is what you want!?!

{Montego} I'm sure Elm! Make it happen, and I want it done before the week is out! Today is Wednesday, by Friday . . . He should be dead!

{Elm} Alright! How you want him? Shot; Columbian Necktie; or the Buried Alive treatment.

{Montego} Elm, surprise me. Long as if it's not carried out around here! Don't need that kind of heat.

{Elm} Ok it's a done deal! I hope his insurance is paid up, cause Friday by 5pm. He'll be talking to St. Peter.

{Montego} Sounds good to me!

{Back at the police station. Holman's team are gearing up. For the challenge of the Meadows Crew takedown!}

{DT Holman} Hey! Hey! Operation takedown is underway.

{DT Shultz} I hear that Holman. So, Williams did you get any information from the informant?

{Officer Williams} No not yet! I told the informant to hold until I give the word. The only thing I want is information.

{DT Holman} Yes! Just street info. We'll pick from time to time. Until someone cracks and believe me! Someone is going to crack!

{Officer Peele} We're going to take that crew down!

{Officer Cole} Yeah, but they are no joke! If you don't know they background! You better check them out thoroughly!

{DT Holman} Yeah that Paul Meadows, and his crew are military trained Marine Corps!

{Officer Holland} Well you picked the right ones for this type of mission.

{DT Holman} Yes! It's going to take military trained cops; to take down military trained crooks. There's nothing that The Meadows Crew can do or say that will keep them from slipping through the cracks anymore! Soon Paul, your ass belongs to me!

(DT Schultz} Hey! I said it before, and I'll say it again! When you're going up against Paul Meadows. You better know what you're doing!

{DT Holman} Oh yeah, because this time; there's no stopping us now! From catching the infamous Paul Meadows and His crew!

{Officer Peele} Now we got the profile to go by on Paul Meadows. So, what are we going to do first!?!

{DT Holman} Hang tight! Cause when we run down on Paul. I want to run down his whole Mother Freaking Crew, and there's not a damn thang they can do about it!

CHAPTER 13

5 STAR RATING DISAPPEARANCE

A Deadly Ordeal

{Malachi is taking a trip but has no idea. What's coming his way!}

{Malachi} I'm going to call Paul. To let him know that the shipment will be a day late.

{Paul receives a call from Malachi.}

{Paul} Hello? Oh Malachi! What's going on? Is everything going as planned with the shipment?

{Malachi} Well that's what I'm calling you about. It seems that the shipment will be a day late.

{Paul} A day late!?! Malachi! You know I run a tight schedule here. I don't have time for delays!

{Malachi} I know Paul, but this is not my fault! I thought everything was on point.

{Paul} Don't think Dammit! Know the shit for sure! Before you make any finalized dates! Kalpesh!

{Malachi} Whoa! Whoa! Whoa! Paul . . . You don't need to be blaming me for the delay. Besides, I am not steering the damn ship! So, watch yourself Paul!

{Paul} Malachi! You been messing around on these shipment orders.

{Malachi} Paul, you have got to understand about my part of the business!

{Just then a knock came at the door.}

{Malachi} Paul hold on, there's someone at the door. Who is it!?!

{Malachi opens the door to see a package on the floor.}

{Malachi} Hey Paul, I'm going to call you back later.

{Paul} Yeah, and don't be long!

{Malachi} Right, right! I won't Paul, later. Now I wonder what's in this package?

{Malachi opens the package, and it explodes!}

{An incoming call for Montego}

{Montego} Hello?

{Elm} Hello Montego! Before I tell you; what I must tell you. I got to ask you. Uhm . . . What time is it?

{Montego} It's 4:55pm Why!?!

{Elm} Well mission accomplished. I said before 5'o clock it would be a done deal right!?!

{Montego} Yes, and that you did say.

{Elm} Done deal!

{Montego} You need to get over here to my office pronto!

{Elm} On my way now!

{Paul} I wonder when Malachi is calling me back? It's been about 30 mins. I'm trying to call him. I hope everything is alright!?! Come on Malachi pick up the phone.

{Paul calls for Malachi, but no answer.}

{Lavis} Okay Paul! So, when are you planning that Baltimore ride?

{Paul} Soon Lavis, but first I'm concerned about this shipment that suppose to be coming in! Malachi tells me that it's going to be late.

{Kym} Delayed, but not denied Paul! The shipment will be on time. Even if it's a little late. No matter what! People will still get what they are looking for.

{Samantha} They certainly will! That fine China is in high demand. North and South Carolina are looking for it as well.

{Lavis} I bet they are! Paul you realize that just about the entire East Coast we got it on lockdown! Also moving strong in the South.

{Paul} Yes, I realized that; and more is still to come. We got to take care of the problem we have in Baltimore! But what is keeping Malachi from calling me back!?!

More, and More Lethal by the Minute.

{Samantha} You know what Paul. I'm going to be the one to lure them Southsiderz to surface.

{Paul} How you plan to do that?

{Samantha} Simple, but first you got to contact Montego, and he'll contact Max, his brother; and they're cousin. For a trip they'll never return from!

{Paul} So you want to do a dinner flight?

{Samantha} No! A trip, as a matter of fact. What about that hydrochloric acid routine. Clean as a whistle.

{Paul} Perfect! That will clean up their acts. Permanently!

{Lavis} Now how are we; going to get them to the place of no return?

{Paul} Once I contact Montego; it's a done deal! But, where the hell is Malachi!?!

{Meanwhile back at Malachi's place. The fire department, and the detectives are there with the bomb squad!}

{DT Holman} Fire Chief what do you got!?!

{Fire Chief} What we had here; was an explosion. According to the extents of the damage. Boxed C4 or a remote bomb like mercury switches!

{DT Shultz} Looks like a professional hit to me.

{DT Holman} Sure do, but by who!?! They knew when; where; and how to go about it!

{DT Peele} You wouldn't suspect the Meadows Crew had anything to do with this!?!

{DT Holman} I don't think so! Hell, we didn't crack the Daniels Disappearance case yet!

{Fire Chief} Well one things for sure. We have one dead guy, and his name is Malachi! And he's not on the choir's roll call list!

{DT Holman} Oh really!?!

{Fire Chief} Yep, and he sure ain't no saint!

{While the Detectives, and the first responders are on the scene at Malachi's. Paul and his crew are working on the plan for the Southsiderz.}

{Paul} Where the hell is Malachi!?! This fool hasn't call back yet! I'm going to call Montego. Maybe he can reach Malachi.

{Paul calls Montego.}

{Montego} Hello?

{Paul} Montego! Hey, this is Paul. Listen did you talk to Malachi this afternoon? I spoke with him a little while ago, and he was supposed to call me back. But I haven't heard from yet. He needs to get back in contact with me!

{Montego} I don't think Malachi will be calling anybody anymore!

{Paul} What do you mean Montego!?! Do you know something that I don't!?!

{Montego} He had to leave in a hurry! So, his people gave him a K Booming Style Party!

{Paul} Oh, a K Booming Style Party huh!?!

{Montego} Yeah! It was the bomb ass party! Everyone toasted to his departure! He was so overwhelmed. The whole shebang just blew his mind!

{Paul} Well that explains the delay for him calling me back. Damn! But look, we're coming out there. Shawn is ready to bring us. It's about the south end again!

{Montego} Alright! I'll fill you in on what's happening, when you guys get here.

{Paul} Good! We're on our way! See you in a few hours.

{Montego} Good deal! We'll take care of these Southsiderz once and for all!

{Paul} Yeah! Because they are going to be, a done deal!

Getting Ready for the Takeout

{Richard} Hey babe, how are you feeling?

{Patricia} I'm feeling fine. I just want to get these procedures started. The sooner; the better.

{Dr. Reeves calls Patricia for her first appointment of consultation.}

{Dr. Reeves} Hello Patricia, this is Dr. Reeves. I'm scheduling you an appointment on Friday in the morning. Can you make it at 10:30am?

{Patricia} Yes Dr. Reeves that will be just fine for 10:30am. This is for the consultation, right?

{Dr. Reeves} Correct! Just for the discussion.

{Patricia} Very well Doctor, we will see you then.

{Richard} Ok so, everything is for Friday at 10:30am. I'll be right there!

{George asking the doctors questions about Brandon.}

{George} Hey Doc. How is Brandon doing!?!

{Doctor} Well Brandon is out of surgery, but still unconscious. It's still touch and go with him. At this present state he can slip into a coma. Reasons why we must stay on top of his condition.

{George} How soon could I be getting out of here?

{Doctor} Don't rush yourself! Take it easy and relax.

{George} Ok Doc! I'll take it easy!

{Officer Peele gets the memo that two of the Meadows Crew is in the Vanderbilt Hospital.}

{DT Holman} Yeah! What is it Detective Peele!?!

{Officer Peele} I just got the memo, that two of the Meadows Crew are in the hospital.

{DT Holman} Which one!?!

{Officer Peele} The Vanderbilt!

{Paul} Shawn! Is my plane ready?

{Shawn} Yes sir! She's all ready for takeoff. Where we're heading Mr. Meadows?

{Paul} Baltimore and spare the turbo boost in flight. Kalpesh!

{Shawn} I have you there in a couple of hours!

{Paul calls Montego to set things up for the Southsiderz!}

{Paul} Hey Montego! Look we should be there at the airport in two hours. So be there in 1 point 45!

{Montego} Got'cha, see you guys then!

{Paul} Oh yeah! Just one more thing.

{Montego} What's that?

{Paul} Bring the Hydro A's!

{Montego} What for!?!

{Paul} Don't ask no questions! Just bring it. We got cleaning up to do. Kalpesh!

{Montego} Cool!

{They arrive at the airport on time, and so do Montego.}

{Montego} Paul and his merry crew! I got the hydrochloric acid. So, now what? Getting ready to clean up the Southsiderz messy lifestyle.

{Samantha} Yes! Call them Montego. I'm ready to smell skin boiling.

{Montego calls Max; Tony, and Mitchell. For meeting at the North end building.}

{Montego} Paul! This is what we're going to do. Samantha will greet them fools for the first, and the last time. Then they'll get a knockout drink, and then . . . Everybody into the pool, of hydrochloric acid.

{Paul} Splendid! Wait a minute . . . Is that them right there!?!

{Montego} Yep! That's them!

{Paul} Alright! It's showtime, and it's not the Apollo!

Triple Patty Melt to Go!

{Montego} Hello fellas. How're things going on the south end?

{Max} Things are going very well on the Southside of town! Ain't that right fam!?!

{Tony} Damn right cuz! Our side of town!

{Mitchell} You better believe it! Nobody's stepping in on our turf, and I mean Nobody!

{Montego} I hear ya' fellas! Loud and clear. Hey look, I have some champagne over here.

{Max} Champagne!?! For what are we celebrating?

{Montego} For your new success. As I hear you guys took out two of the members of the competition.

{Tony} Yep! Just me and cuz. We rolled up on those fools. Ask them a few questions. Next thing they knew, guns were in their faces.

{Mitchell} Right! Right! I told their punk asses to turn and face the wall! That's when we popped them. Pow! Pow!

{Montego} Shot them square in the back huh?

{Max} Yeah, and that's how we do! Well, since we're on the subject. Why all the questions man!?!

{Montego} Nothing, but I was curious on how's that champagne doing for you guys?

{The three answered simultaneously} All good!

{Montego} Oh fellas, by the way! A friend of mine wanted to meet you guys. Come on out Paul!

{Paul} Hello fellas, glad to finally meet you guys!

{They looked astonished at Montego, and in disbelief.}

{Max} Montego! What the hell is this man? Who the hell is he!?!

{Paul} The name is Meadows, Paul Meadows; and you guys . . . Has crossed me for the last time!

{Max and his boys get a little antsy, but weary at same time.}

{Max} Man! You set us up! You roll with this cat don't you!?!

{Montego} Indeed I do. This is what happens when you step on territories. Where you don't belong! I told you Max; the last time we spoke. Remember! I tried to cut you guys a deal, but you refused. Then if that wasn't bad enough. You guys rolled up and shot two of our guys! Are you stupid, or what!?!

{Tony} We did what we had to do! So, you two old fogies can kiss our asses!

{Paul} You know, I've seen some Stupid; Crazy; Idiotic people in my time. But you guys Takes the cake!

{Mitchell} Max! Let's take these fools they ain't about nothing!

{Paul} Huh! Before you guys become real ignorant! Just turn around and look behind you.

{The three turns around to see Meadows Crew pointing their guns at them, but suddenly the three passes out.}

{Paul} Ok Montego, where's the hydrochloric acid?

{Montego} Downstairs in the concrete graves. Deep enough for them to have their own slots.

{Paul} Good! Get them down there and dump them immediately!

{Samantha} Yes sir! They'll be clean as a whistle! Ha-ha!

{Kym} I told that little fart the last time we met! Don't mess with the Meadows Crew!

{Porshia} Now look at them! Matter of fact, drop them bitches now!

{As Max; Tony; and Mitchell's limp bodies were dumped in acid, and their flesh are bubbling and melting away. Paul just stands over the concrete graves. As the singe and steam eats away at them. Paul turns to the crew and says.}

{Paul} When we get crossed; we don't negotiate! We capture and consolidate. The ones who crossed us! Then it's time for a disappearing act. I'm going to say like Snoop Dogg . . . Those Nizzels are Sizzled for Rizzle! So, bye Bitchels!

Look Before You Leap

{Montego} Ok Paul, now that the Southsiderz has been neutralized. We can start focusing on the shipments.

{Paul} How can we focus on the shipments; when our middle man is . . .

{Montego} No longer with us!

{Paul} What do you mean by; no longer with us?

{Kym} Sounds like what he said! No longer with us. The question is! Ii he Dead or Alive?

{Montego} Very much dead! Let's just say. He's was blown away. Kaboom!

{Paul} Damn Montego! I told you to wait. At least until the next shipment came in. Now how we going to receive the shipment without Malachi in place?

{Montego} Don't worry Paul. I've been working on that angle for a few months now. Believe me when I tell you. Malachi was on his way out! I just helped him out, a little bit.

{Kym} Malachi . . . You helped him out alright! Right out of his own lifetime!

{The crew laughs}

{Paul} Ok Montego! So, how are we going to get the shipment, without any altercations!?!

{Montego} You got the money?

{Paul} Damn straight we got the money! Down to the last penny.

{Montego} Alright, then it's time for us to deal without the middle man.

{Kym} Oh well, it's process of elimination.

{Back at the station. Holman and his division are getting ready to investigate the site where Paul had purchased.}

{DT Holman} Alright crew listen up! You guys know we're after the notorious Meadows Crew. After all; we have reasons to believe that Mr. Daniel's not only missing, but he was murdered! Because how can anyone just disappear without a trace; clue; or something!

{DT Shultz} Don't worry about it What's in the dark, will come to light! You can run, but you can't hide!

{Officer Peele} Every step they take. Every move they make, and all the laws the break, we'll be watching them!

{DT Holman} So, now we're quoting lyrics from The Police!?!

{Officer Peele} Oh Damn my bad, Huh I thought we were the police, and I'm not talking about the rock group featuring Sting. When we catch their asses; they going to know they been stung!

{The officers Just laughed.}

{Officer Frye} You're right Peele! They sure going to be stung hard!

{DT Holman} Well we need something, or someone that seen; heard or even know something. To come forth with some concrete evidence. That can convict and put their asses away!

{DT Shultz} Detective Holman, what did you just say!?!

{DT Holman} I said, that will convict their . . .

{DT Shultz} No-no-no! Second to the last thing you said!?!

{DT Holman} What!?! Come forth with some . . .

{Both Holman and Shultz say at the same time.} Concrete evidence!

{DT Shultz} Yeah! What type of business do Paul do again!?!

{DT Holman} Realtor/Concrete business. He also manufactures school supplies, and fabrics.

{DT Shultz} That's what I thought you said he do! If a Notorious Mobster want to make someone disappear? What did they use to do? {All the officers said simultaneous.} Cement shoes!

CHAPTER 14

PASSION FOR THE PAIN

Pain by the Pound

{Richard calls George. To check on him and Brandon.}

{George} Hello.

{Richard} Hey George what's going on!?! How you feeling bro?

{George} Sore as hell, but I'm making it.

{Richard} Good! Good! How is Brandon doing?

{George} Oh you didn't hear about Brandon. Well according by what the doctors are saying, that Brandon is in a coma. That's why it's touch and go with him.

{Richard} Damn! When was the last time Paul, or any of the others came by to see you guys?

{George} It's been a few days since I've seen any of those guys! But knowing them; they probably went to Baltimore to handle some business! If you know what I mean!?!

{Richard} Yeah, I know.

{Patricia} Richard; who are you talking to sweetie?

{Richard} I'm talking to George babe. He's telling me that Brandon is in a coma.

{Patricia} They don't know if he's going to pull through, or not!

{George} Hey look, Richard! I'll talk to you later. The doctor is coming in now. Hope to see you soon.

{Richard} Sure thing, and don't worry! We're going to come by to see you guys.

{George} Cool I'll see you guys soon.

{Richard} Alright bro! You take it easy and get some rest!

{Meanwhile Paul and Montego went to meet the distributors to make the deal for the shipment.}

{Paul} Montego! I hope you ready for this? Because being without Malachi, they may not trust it.

{Montego} It doesn't matter about Malachi! Hell; he wasn't doing like he was supposed to in the first place! Besides; we got this!

{Now Paul and Montego, leaves to meet the pilots at the airport. For the incoming shipment.}

{Paul} Alright Montego! Now that we're the only ones riding out to the airport. What really happened to Malachi?

{Montego} Are you sure you want to know what happened to Malachi!?!

{Paul} Hell; I asked, didn't I?

{Montego} Remember the last time you spoke with Malachi over the phone!?!

{Paul} Yeah, I remember. So, what happened?

{Montego} I hired a contract killer to take him out. By any means necessary. So, I know you heard on the news about an apartment exploded on the North side of town.

{Paul} That was Malachi's apartment wasn't it!?!

{Montego} Damn straight! Lit his ass like match on fire. Good old mercury switch with some C4. Gift wrapped nice and pretty for him. The hitman made and delivered it to the door step. Malachi opens it and kaboom!

{Paul} Damn! I thought I was lethal. I almost don't have anything on you.

{Montego} Dang! Are you sure about that Paul!?!

{Paul} Hey, hey! Notice I said, "Almost anything!" Well we're here now. You ready?

{Montego} Man, I was born ready. Let's go!

{They exit the car and greets the pilots.}

{Paul} Welcome to our lovely city.

{Pilot 1} Thanks, but let's get down to business. You guys got the money!?!

{Paul} Sure thing! We wouldn't be here if we didn't.

{Pilot 2} Uh where's Malachi? He is the one who meets us.

{Montego} Well Malachi won't be meeting anyone anymore! Due to an unexplainable fire explosion. That happened at his apartment.

{Pilot 1} What!! How that happened!?!

{Montego} Not sure, but according to the news they stated that. He was at home, but a package was delivered to the address. He must've opened the package then boom!

{Pilot 2} That's a damn shame! No remorse neither!?! Damn he was a brother from another mother to me. Swear I better not find out who killed him!

{Paul} I feel you my man, but let's get down to business. You guys got the stuff?

{Pilot 1} Yep, All here!

{Paul} Well then, let's deal! $750,000 dollars. Cash or Debit!?!

{Pilot 2} Cash my man! Cash!

{Paul} Oh well, cash it is! First the stuff then the money.

{Montego}Damn straight! All that Snow, and that Fine China!

{Pilot 1} We got everything you want, and then some. Well my friend, it was great doing business with you. Paul, Montego! Until next time. Adios Amigo's!

{Montego} See ya! Now see Paul! We could handle this ourselves!

{Paul} I guess you're right Montego. Surely save me some money!

Better Deal Days

{Kym calls Jason. To see how things are going at the warehouse.}

{Jason} Hi Kym, how are you and the rest of the crew doing?

{Kym} Huh, we're fine! Just talking care of business. So, what's going on down at the warehouse! Are the fabrics moving like clockwork?

{Jason} The fabrics are doing well, and the school supplies are going well also. So, this evening; are you free. Or are you busy?

{Kym} Well! Looks like I'm free, and willing to be opened! If you catch my drift?

{Jason} Well I want to catch your drift!

{Kym} Good! Have the documents ready to show this evening. I will be there around 6pm.

{Jason} See you then. And oh yeah, just one more thing Ms. Lei!

{Kym} What's that?

{Jason} No police.

{The both just laughed! Now as for the police. They're on the move to the new site where Paul had purchased.}

{DT Holman} Ok guys listen up! We're at Paul's building site. To Investigate and ask questions about the Daniel's Disappearance Case!

{DT Shultz} So, just asking questions, and investigating?

{DT Holman} Yes! Hopefully we can get some answers out of someone!

{Officer Peele} We're going in here with expectations of facts and results!

{Officer Williams} Ok y'all let's roll!

{The Officers goes in the building to see what they can find.}

{DT Holman} Hello anybody here!?!

{Officer Peele} Looks like no one's here.

{DT Shultz} Well this place is still under construction, and they are still working on the place.

{Officer Williams} We got so much to investigate. The Daniel's Case; Malachi's Case. I mean damn! Do you guys think that Paul Meadows is behind this mess!?!

{DT Holman} I'm not sure, but I won't doubt it though! The truth shall reveal itself.

{DT Shultz} Ah Holman look at here, I'm going to make a call, and I'll be right back!

{Shultz walks out to make a call.}

{DT Shultz} Hey! You got the 411 before they get there! Ok good! Long as you don't get caught! Look I got to go. I hit you up later.

{DT Holman} I just don't get it Peele! It seems like when we get a moment to move in on Paul. Something always either blocks us, or hints to him to not be there.

{Officer Peele} Yeah it is strange.

{DT Shultz} Ok I just spoke to the informant, Paul is out of town on business, but he's going to be at the warehouse tomorrow.

{Samantha} How soon can we get back on vacation? Since we were interrupted with the unwelcome news.

{Lavis} Well I want to make sure our guys are alright first, and then we can get back to our vacay getaway.

{Rachel} Porshia, you know we must go back to Georgia so, we can meet up with Selena.

{Porshia} We do, for what?

{Rachel} To ensure that the supplies are moving like clockwork. We have no room for errors, or any more surprise!

{Porshia} Alright is Paul or Montego going as well?

{Rachel} I don't know, but I seriously doubt it.

{At that warehouse. Kym meets with Jason to discuss business matters, and other things as well.}

{Kym} Jason! How are you doing down here? Do you have the documents?

{Jason} Yes, I do lovely lady. Here's they are: The Documents; Spreadsheets; Profit and Loss Sheets, and me too.

{Kym} Ok, first the documents, and then you. Well everything looks to be in place. Any plans for the weekend?

{Jason} Yes, if you're accompanying me to dinner, and a movie afterwards.

{Kym} Well with an offer like that how can I refuse?

{Jason} You can't, just accept it.

{Both of them kissed passionately.}

Joy, Along with the Pain.

{Paul and Montego are in route back to the office to discuss about future moves.}

{Montego} Now you see just how easy that was!?! To get this product ourselves, and without Malachi!

{Paul} Ok! So, you may have done your homework with Malachi, and the connections for the shipments. Next time, wait for my signal. We don't need to be making any hasty decisions!

{Montego} Sure thing boss! So, are you sending the ladies back to Georgia?

{Paul} Yes! We got to make sure everything is going like it's supposed to down there. I got to send them in incognito mode. To make sure they stay safe.

{Montego} Ok, are we going as well? Cause you know we're two men short!

{Paul} Don't you worry about that! I have people all over the place. Trust me they good! As soon as they step of the plane. I have protection for them!

{Montego} What kind of protection you talking about?

{Paul} Mercenaries kind of protection. That fortified trained killer kind of protection! Anybody or anything comes within a 20-yard radius of them, that'll bring harm to them. Will be popped off and eliminated! No questions asked.

{Montego} Doggone Paul, 20-Yards!?! Hell, how many of them?

{Paul} That I will not tell my friend!

{Montego} Ok, how many of the crew you sending? Just Rachel and Porshia.

{Paul} I'm going to check with Richard as well, and I believe Kym will go. Samantha and Lavis I'm not so sure about those two.

{Paul contacts Richard}

{Paul} Hey Richard how is everything going with your wife?

{Richard} Everything's fine, just at the doctor's office with my wife. She's starting her treatments today. What's up!?!

{Paul} Well I was calling you to see if you were going to take that trip to Georgia with the crew?

{Richard} No I'm not going to be taking that flight. I'm taking care of my wife, until she's better! Then I'll let you know! Ok Paul.

{Paul} Alright Richard! Take care of the wife. I'll talk to you later.

{Richard} Good deal!

{Detectives Holman and Shultz just received an anonymous tip about the Daniel's case.

{DT Holman} Shultz, listen to this!

{Holman plays back a recording of Daniels last phone call conversation!}

{DT Shultz} Oh really!?! So, he was talking to Ms. Kym about a dinner date. Before he went missing.

{DT Holman} Yes, and if that's the case . . . then we were questioning the wrong person!

{Officer Williams} You guys just coming to that conclusion? You should've been questioned Kym Lei, not Jason!

{DT Shultz} Yeah! You see Holman; I told you! Before you start messing around with the Meadows Crew. You better know what you're doing.

{DT Holman} Well got damn who side are you on Shultz!?!

{Officer Peele} Damn straight, I was wondering the same thing myself.

{DT Shultz} You know I'm on your side Holman! But you got to know what you're doing. When you're freaking around with the Meadows Crew!

{DT Holman} I know one things for sure, we better get Ms. Kym, because she knows what happened to Mr. Daniels in this case.

Kym's & Jason Passion Through the Pain

{Kym} Oh Jason! We're going to Georgia with the ladies. So, we'll know how the merchandise, and product is moving.

{Jason} So, you mean to tell me that, we are going to Georgia!?! Me and you!

{Kym} Yes! You, myself and the other ladies. Oh, by the way . . . You know how to work with guns?

{Jason} Yes, I certainly do. In this business I better know how to use a gun!

{Kym} Good! So, we'll be leaving tomorrow morning, but until then. It's me and you now.

{Jason} Well in that case, bring yourself on over here to me right now!

{While Jason and Kym find themselves in a bliss heated passion! Rachel and Porshia are going to the hospital to see how Brandon and George are doing.}

{Rachel} Well hello George, and how feeling today? Better I hope!

{George} I'm alright. Ready to get the hell up, and out of here! You ladies went to check on Brandon today?

{Porshia} No not yet, but we're going to lay our eyes on him. Has he revived from his coma?

{George} Not to my knowledge! Boy, when we get out of here. Those guys who shot us in the back is going to pay dearly!

{Rachel} Shush your mouth George! You don't won't to give it away!

{George} Give what away?

{Porshia} What she means is; that has already been handled. Don't have to worry about them anymore.

{George} Oh! So, that means their no longer around Huh!?!

{Rachel} Quiet is to be kept! Not amongst the living.

{Porshia} Shush! Quiet guys, we're in a hospital you know.

{George} True that Porshia! So, what's next?

{Rachel} Georgia is what's next. We must check on the status of the merchandise. School supplies; Fabrics; and other products as well.

{Rachel turns to look at Porshia and George and gives a wink.}

{Paul is keeping tabs on everything, making sure there's no room for errors!}

{Paul} Hello Lavis, this is Paul! I'm going to need you and Samantha to partake on this trip to Georgia!

{Lavis} Paul! Samantha and I need this time to . . .

{Paul} It's not request Lavis! It's a Damn requirement! Now I need you two, to be on that plane tomorrow morning. Is that clear!?!

{Lavis} Alright Paul! You're the boss! We'll be there, but after this trip! Me and Sam are on break!

{Paul hangs up the phone before Lavis could finish his sentence.}

{Lavis} Now why Paul can run down on us!?! But he won't speak to Richard like that! How come Sam, how come!?!

{Samantha} Paul feels like he can bae! That's why. People only can do what they are allowed to do. We create, what we allow! In any and everything we do. Good, Bad; The Ugly, or Indifferent!

{Meanwhile back at the police station.}

{DT Holman} Officer Peele and Williams. Look I need you guys to go to the warehouse, and check things out over there.

{Officer Peele} No problem we got it! Ok Williams let's go!

{Officer Williams} Alright we're gone!

{DT Holman} Alright Shultz! You roll with me.

{DT Shultz} Where we going Holman!?!

{DT Holman} To Paul's office! To see what he got up his sleeve. Officer Hart; Cole; and Frye! You guys checkout Daniel's place for clues!

{The officers shouted out} Yes Sir!

{DT Holman} Shultz, let's roll!

Sabotage Is Such A Pain in the Ass!

{Paul calls for his crew. To meet at the airport for take-off to Georgia.}

{Paul} Hello Porshia, this is Paul. Get in touch with Rachel. The time has come to go to Georgia.

{Porshia} Well she's right here with me, talking to George.

{George} That's Paul, let me speak to him! What's going on Paul!?!

{Paul} Just getting the crew ready for the Georgia trip. I wish you and Brandon were joining the ladies on this venture.

{George} Oh don't worry! I'm coming home soon. So, I'll be back in action again.

{Paul} George when you come home. You are going to rest yourself! So, you can fully recover.

{George} Oh ok I understand! As for the ones who did this to me and Brandon. They been handled huh!?!

{Paul} What you think?

{George} Well ok here's Rachel!

{Rachel} I'm here Paul. What's up?

{Paul} Ok Rachel, now the time has come to handle that business in Georgia! I want you to get in contact with Kym. To let her know what's going on. I already spoke with Lavis and Samantha. To meet you guys at the airport by 9am.

{Rachel} Ok! I'm going to get on the horn with Kym now! So, we can all meet up simultaneously.

{Paul} Good! When you guys land. I have a security team out there. Just because my guys aren't going. Doesn't mean you ladies won't be protected. You know me better than that right?

{Rachel} What do you mean Paul? What security team!?!

{Paul} You'll see when you guys land. Let me know when y'all get to the airport.

{Rachel} Ok, will do Paul.

{The crew is gathering up for the Georgia flight, but Detectives Holman and Shultz arrives at Paul's office.}

{DT Holman} Officer Peele this is Holman come back!

{Officer Peele} Go head Holman.

{DT Holman} Me and Shultz just arrived at Paul's Office! I want you, and Williams to search their warehouse and I mean search it good! You guys got the warrants?

{Officer Peele} We got it! What are we looking for though precisely?

{DT Holman} Any type of clues! Like shipment invoices; documents of transactions. Drugs; Guns; anything we can pin against him. Even tax forms.

Also, any track records that can lead to murders, and people that disappeared.

{Officer Peele} I seriously doubt if we find anything like that, but we'll look anyhow!

{DT Shultz} So, what are we going to do about Paul?

{DT Holman} I'm going to have a talk with Paul Meadows. But I want you to do a little rewiring with Paul's car.

{DT Shultz} I know you not talking about sabotaging his car!?!

{DT Holman} Yes! That's exactly what I'm talking about!

{DT Shultz} Damn I thought you pull some crazy stunt to try to stop Paul, but nothing like this! Seriously Holman!?!

{DT Holman} Look, make like Nike, and Just Do It! Thank you so much! Just in case he makes a run for it!

{DT Shultz} Now I know one thing for sure about Paul. He ain't running from nothing, including the police! Like I said before, and I'm going to say it again. When you're messing with Paul Meadows, you better know what you're doing!

CHAPTER 15

TAKE THE PRESSURE

No Problem at All

{The crew meets up at the airport, and boards the plane, but waiting on Kym to arrive.}

{Shawn} What's going on Meadows Crew!?! Ready for another flight, and where to this time?

{Lavis} Georgia! To the ATL!

{Kym} So Jason, now you get to go with us on one our business trips.

{Jason} Yes! So, what we need to do when we all land!?!

{Kym} Well, I will fill you in on that info; when we get on the plane.

{Just then Officers Peele and Williams approaches Kym and Jason.}

{Officer Peele} Well hello Ms. Kym, I presume!

{Jason} Oh my Damn! Not these guys again! Seems like we'll never get rid of these clowns. Hell, Ringling Brothers and Barlem & Bailey Circus went out business, and I think I know why! Too many of their employees were playing hooky from work. Damn I see y'all costumes, but where's your make up!?!

{Kym} Exactly babe, and what can we do for the Blues Brothers today? If we had the time and in which we don't!

{Officer Peele} Oh I do believe Ms. Kym, that you will have plenty of time for us today.

{Kym} What you mean!?! I have somewhere to be and you guys are holding us up!

{Officer Williams} More than you realize Ms. Kym, more than you realize. We're taking you in for questioning.

{Jason} More like interrogating.

{Officer Peele} Yeah whatever works! As long as we find what we're looking for.

{Kym} Well what is it that you're looking for?

{Officer Williams} Answers, about Mr. Daniel's disappearance case! We have reasons to believe that, you know what happened to him.

{Jason} So, what does that mean? You guys don't have any proof of the speculations.

{Officer Williams} Because she was the last person who spoke to and seen Mr. Daniels before he went missing!

{Meanwhile back at the airport. The crew is starting to wonder, if Kym is going to be on time for the trip.}

{Rachel} Well damn where's Kym!?! She was supposed to be here, basically meeting us here!

{Porshia} I know right! She's late, this is not like her! Kym is always before time. Something must've happened for her not to be here.

{Shawn} I hope she's on the way, or something! Give a call Ms. Kym!

{Rachel} I'm calling her right now! To see what's keeping her!?!

{Rachel call Kym's phone, but there's no answer! Just going to voicemail.}

{Lavis} We're running late, and we have to be in Georgia by 1pm.

{Samantha} Yes, and we all know Paul don't want no lateness!

{Rachel} I don't know what's going on with Kym, but we got to go. I'm going to call Paul. To let him know what's happening! Hello Paul?

{Paul} Yes Rachel, what's going on?

{Rachel} Paul! Kym is not here, and we all been waiting for thirty minutes now! Shall we proceed without her?

{Paul} What!?! You called her, or has anyone contacted her?

{Rachel} I've been trying to call her, but no luck!

{Paul} Okay! It's getting late! So, you guys better take off. Because Selena is expecting you guys around 1. Don't worry about Kym. I'll find out what happened to her. You guys go ahead. She'll more than likely come after you guys get to Selena.

{Rachel} Okay Paul, we're out! Shawn take off! Next stop Georgia!

{Porshia} So we leaving Kym!?!

{Rachel} Yeap! Paul told me we got to go! Kym will probably be there after us.

TIME IS OF THE ESSENCE

{Richard and Patricia are waiting for Dr. Reeves to bring the results.)

{Dr. Reeves} Okay Patricia I have the results and according them we're on the right track. If you continue doing what you've been doing, the cancer cells can be eliminated.

{Richard} That's great news Doc! So how many more treatments she has to go through?

{Dr. Reeves} Well it's still early yet, but things are looking good from this stand point. Tomorrow at 10am. I would like for you to have chemo treatment; and I believe within these next few treatments. You should be cancer free!

{Patricia} Yes! I can't wait to get that report!

{Richard} Yes, me too bae! I already heard the news. We just got to catch up with the moment! Hey Doc! You're late, why haven't you read the results that my wife's cancer free.

{Paul tries to call Kym, but soon was Interrupted by Holman and Shultz}

{DT Holman} Well hello Paul, and how are you doing today? I take it that you been trying to call Kym huh!?! Well, I hate to be the barer of bad news, but right about now. She's being detained for questioning, about the Daniel's case.

{Paul} You know what Holman; you and your bitch ass cops are really getting on my last nerves! Now I'm going to tell you guys one time, and one time only! Release her right now, or else!

{DT Holman} Or else what? Come on Paul! Tell me something good.

{Paul} You'll find out! Soon enough toy cop!

{DT Holman} Yeah that's what I thought you'd better had said, "Nothing!"

{Down at the station, Kym is being interrogated by the officers.}

{Officer Frye} Hello Ms. Kym, my name is Officer Frye. I'm quite sure you already know why you're here. So, let's get down to business. Kym you were the last person that Daniel spoke with before he went missing. So, what happened!?!

{Kym} Just because I so happen to have spoken with Mr. Daniel before he went missing. Does not mean that I know anything about him missing. Do you know many people in the world goes missing, and how many people they talked to before the unfortunate happen?

{Officer Frye} So what you're saying is you have no idea, no clue! About where Daniel was; who he was with around 7pm on the night of question?

{Kym} No I don't know. The last time I spoke to him, he was supposed to be going out! That's all I know.

{At this point Officers Peele and Williams walked in. To follow up on the interrogations.}

{Paul} Look Holman! Right about now, I'm a very busy man. Oh, I will be getting in touch with your Commissioner! And your department will be hearing from my lawyers, but for now; I bid for you a bit of Goodbye!

{DT Shultz} Holman! We got Kym, so we got what we need, or shall I say who we need. To crack this case wide open! Paul, watch yourself! Cause we're coming for you real soon.

{Paul} I'm so looking forward to it! But in the meantime, Bye Bitches!

Morning Flight to Georgia

{Lavis} We'll be landing in Georgia soon.

{Samantha} Yeah, to do what there!?! Besides looking at Selena.

{Rachel} I know Samantha, I'm not used to going on these ventures without Kym.

{Porshia} I second the motion! She's sought of the leader of the pack. Well maybe she'll be following behind us!

{Samantha} I hope so, shoot! Me and Lavis could've been on our vacay getaway!

{Lavis} That's right! I hope nothing's happened to her!?!

{Meanwhile, Paul arrived at the police station to find out what happened to Kym.}

{Paul} Ok where's Ms. Kym?

{Sargent Mayfield} Excuse me Sir, how may I help you?

{Paul} Look, my name is Paul Meadows! I'm here to have Ms. Kym Lei released. She was brought in for questioning.

{Sargent Mayfield} Oh yes! I'll see if she'll be coming out of Interrogations soon, but this can take a while. So, hang tight!

{Paul} There is no hanging tight! I'm here to have her released at once! Or would you rather talk to my Lawyers! Now, which one you guys prefer!?!

{Officer Frye} Well, Mr. Paul Meadows! We had a feeling you would show up to spring your girl out!

{Paul} You Damn Straight! I'm here to spring her out of here! It doesn't matter. Either way she's getting the Hell out of here!

{At this time Detectives Holman and Shultz walks in on the scene.}

{DT Holman} Ok Paul, what brings you down here? Oh . . . Yes! Your precious Lil' Kym! Well major boss man, she's being questioned about the Daniel's Disappearance Case, or unless You . . . Can shed a little light on the subject.

{Paul} Look! Once again, she doesn't know anything about Daniels Disappearance.

We all want to know what happened to Mr. Daniels.

{Just then Kym is walking out from the interrogations room.}

{George} Hey Doc!?! When am I scheduled to get out of here!?! I'm ready to go home and get in my bed!

{Doctor} Well, if your temperature stays at the normal level by 3o'clock this afternoon. Then we can discharge you. But we will see how you're doing by then.

Because we can be held accountable if we discharge you too early, and you'll right back here again!

{George} Okay Doc! I've been here for a couple of weeks. I'm ready to go home. Hell, back to work is more like it! By the way How's Brandon doing!?! Has he waking from his coma yet?

{Doctor} As a matter of fact, he woke up; but he drifted back out again. He's in and out of consciousness. So, he'll be coming back for good. I believe so! Besides, his vitals are good.

{George} Thank GOD! Ah! He's so Awesome! I know I'm getting out of here now!

{Back in Georgia with the crew.}

{Rachel} So, now that we're here, where's Selena? She knew we're coming, and she supposed to be right here before us.

{Lavis} Well here she comes now! Not a moment too soon!

{Selena} Welcome Meadows! Step lively as you guys exits the plane. If you look to your left, you notice the soldiers are ready for anything. If you look to your right. At the top of the hangers, expert sharpshooters are in place. If anyone was to seem like a threat! It's over for them, or shall I say curtains baby!

{Samantha} Who had all this setup!?!

{Selena} Paul of course! Well let's go!

{Porshia} Damn! Highly trained snipers huh!?!

{Rachel} Alright then let's get it!

FAITH X WORKS = RESULTS

{Patricia} Well babe! Today I'll be taking my final examination. To see if the cancer is gone.

{Richard} Yes! Let's pray for that miracle of Healing! Thank you, Father GOD for this Blessed day, YOU allowed us to see! For YOU are Worthy! So Worthy to be Praised! Father GOD; We come to You Humbly as we know how! We Plead; Declare, and Decree! The Blood of JESUS on wife's Healing right now! In the Mighty Name of JESUS! We declared Patricia cancer free, and completely restored, In the Name of JESUS! All sickness and diseases must return to the pits of hell; from which it comes from! Yes! In JESUS Name We forever pray! Amen! Amen!! And Amen!!!

{Patricia} Amen! Babe, I know you could pray, but I didn't know can put it down like that! You know what babe, there's a time and a place for everything! Huh, I believe that your time with Paul is soon to end. So, don't be surprised when it does.

{Richard} Well babe, I'm quite sure it will come to an end; but I will not be surprised for it to come to pass!

{Patricia} Well what's that?

{Richard} You know the things that you do. The Good; Bad; Ugly, or Indifferent! Has a way of coming back to you? Like that good old boomerang! What you cast out on the waters, just expect it to return unto you. Maybe with a little extra if you know what I mean!

{Patricia} Well babe right now! Let's believe in the healing process first, then we'll focus on the other stuff later! First things first! I love you babe!

{Richard} I love you too! Always and Forever!

{The two passionately kiss!}

{As Richard and Patricia are on the way to the hospital. Brandon's finally coming around.}

{Brandon} Doctor! Doctor; where am I?

{Brandon spoke vaguely to the nurse monitoring him}

{Nurse} Doctor, uhm doctor! Patient in room 412 is calling for a doctor.

{Doctor} Patient's name!?!

{Nurse} Brandon Wiley. The one that was in the coma.

{Doctor} Oh yes, I'll be there momentarily nurse.

{Nurse} Very well, I will check back with the patient. To make sure he's still conscious! We don't want him to slip back into darkness!

{At the Vanderbilt; great news surpasses!}

{George} Well Doc! 3o'clock and all is well with me! My temperature has been normal for two days. So, Doc, what's the verdict?

{Doctor} Well George my friend, looks like you'll be going home today!

{George} Yes! Finally, I'm out of here! But what about Brandon!?!

{Doctor} Well I have good news to tell about Brandon. He's out of the coma, and he's condition is stable!

{George} Doc that's great! But I bet he's a little weak huh!?!

{Doctor} Actually, quite the opposite. He's very responsive! Just a little confused about how he got here. He doesn't even realize the ordeal he's been through. But in a short period of time, he'll be going home soon as well.

{Meanwhile Richard and Patricia are getting their results from Doctor Reeves!}

{Doctor Reeves} Well Patricia, I have you're results from the labs. And according to the results You are cancer free!

{Patricia} Glory! Hallelujah! Thank you, JESUS! I'm a survivor! It has been no one, but YOU GOD! That saved me from the dreaded disease!

{Richard} Yes sir! Thank You Father GOD! See babe, our faith and HIS Grace!

{Doctor} It's been a blessing throughout the day today!

{Richard} Really Doc? What else happened!?!

{Doctor Reeves} Oh you didn't hear the news, that George is going home today, and Brandon is officially out of the coma, and he's in stable condition! Now won't HE do it!?!

{Both Richard and Patricia shouted, and praised GOD!}

No Need to Wonder Why, Paul is Don!

{Paul} Kym! What did these clowns do to you?

{Kym} Just a whole bunch of questions that they're not going to get answers to!

{Paul} Straight harassing you huh!?! Ok they want to play devious? So, let's play.

{Kym} Yeah! I'm really getting tired of these accusations. Every time I turn around! Still about this Daniel's Disappearance Case!

{Paul} Oh wait, I got something in mind for the questionnaire crew! Something just for them.

{Kym} What you going to do Paul!?! Nothing crazy I hope!

{Paul} Don't worry! I got this as usual!

{Back in Georgia with the crew! Being heavily escorted to the warehouse to check on production.}

{Samantha} You know what Rachel!?! I think Kym and Jason are hooking up.

{Rachel} Well maybe, but we got more important things to work on.

{Samantha} I guess you're right! So, here we are at the warehouse! The production looks fine. So, why are here again!

{Just as the crew was getting settled. The sound of gunshots rings out!}

{Selena} Oh my GOD! Take cover!

{The soldiers battled outside! Firing back on the opposing crew! Spraying shots, in hopes to hit someone!

{Lavis} Damn now I see why we were summonsed to come here! More than likely to protect the product, and inventory. Is everyone strapped!?!

{The crew replied, Hell yeah!}

{Lavis} Alright Meadows . . . Let's rip their asses!

{The Meadows Crew took out their weapons and start firing at the opposing crew from the Westside part of Atlanta!}

{Lavis contacts Paul in the mist of the firing fury!}

{Lavis} Paul! We're in the middle of a war zone! What the Hell you sentence us to death!

{Paul} What!?! A war zone! Ok, remember how it was in Afghanistan? Code verb!

{Lavis} Roger Paul! The firing is coming from the Northeast! At a 75-degree angle and trying to take our Damn heads off!

{Samantha} Selena! Do you have any grenades!?! In any of the crates?

{Selena} Hell no! We have Assault Weapons!

{Samantha} Lavis here! AK-47 babe! Light they're asses up!

{Lavis} Like the 4th of July babe!

{Lavis shoots down eight of them in one swoop! Rat-tat-tat-tat! Humph, and that was that. But the crew was unaware that Porshia was hit by gunfire!}

{Rachel} Lavis! Samantha! Porshia! You guys alright!

{Samantha} Yeah girl we're fine! Selena! Where the hell you at!?! What you trying to do? Set us up with an ambush!

{Selena} Samantha! Why would I want to set you guys up? When I work for y'all!?! Think girlfriend think!

{Rachel} Samantha, Selena ain't trying to set us up. But hey! Where's Porshia!?!

{Selena} Yeah! Where is she? Porshia! Porshia!

{Samantha} Where you at girl!?! You think she's alright? She would've been present by now! Porshia! Oh my GOD! Selena! Lavis! Rachel! Come here quickly! Porshia got hit by gunfire!

{Rachel} What happened to her!?!

{Lavis} What the Hell!

{Samantha} She's been shot! Porshia!

{Rachel} Call 911 Now!

CHAPTER 16

ALWAYS COOL UNDER PRESSURE

If It Ain't One Thing, It's Another.

{The Meadows Crew finds themselves in a 911 situation! That they got to handle themselves!}

{Rachel} I'm calling Paul right now!

{Lavis} We got to get her to the hospital!

{Paul} Rachel, what's going on down there?

{Rachel} Paul! Porshia's been shot! We are getting ready to take her to the hospital! I don't know why you sent us down here?

{Paul} I sent you guys there to ensure the merchandise is moving like clockwork. Not to engage in combat! Lavis tells me, that you guys engaged in war with some Georgia gangsters!

{Rachel} I don't know about any gangsters around here, but all I know is . . . Somebody going to pay the piper!

{Paul} Oh yes! You can bet your bottom dollar that someone is going to pay, and I mean dearly; but I must take care of something first. Then I will have something for our welcoming party.

{Rachel} I hear you loud and clear Paul!

{Samantha} Hurry Rachel! We got to get Porshia to the hospital! There's no time waste!

{Lavis} Yeah! Let's go; pronto!

{The crew takes Porshia to the hospital and praying that they make it in time!}

{George} Doc I thank you for all your help. I'm going to go and check on Brandon. To see how he's doing.

{George is being discharge and going to see Brandon before he goes home.}

{Paul} I need to call Montego and discuss some things with him.

{Paul calls Montego to let him know what's going on in Georgia!}

{Montego} Hey Paul what's up!?!

{Paul} We need to have another meeting. No talking over the phone.

{Montego} Uh oh! Somebody needs Maaco! I'll be there tomorrow morning.

WALKING THE INVISIBLE LINE

{Kym calls Jason, for them to meet at a local restaurant.}

{Jason} Hey Kym and how are you this afternoon? Paul came to get you out of there!

{Kym} Yeah, but I'm really getting sick and tired of those clown ass cops!

{Jason} They're not going to let up! Until they make an arrest for that Daniel's case. So, every chance they get; they'll be harassing us.

{Kym} Not for long they won't!

{Jason} What do you mean by that!?!

{Kym} According to Paul he'll be taking care of them once and all!

{Jason} Don't say another word over the phone! I'll take your word for it! The Lawyers!

{Kym} Yep! With the Commissioner to run down on them toys!

{Meanwhile George is chatting with Brandon to finally see how he's feeling! Knocking at the door.}

{Brandon} Who is it!?!

{George} What's going on bro?

{Brandon} Hey, what's good my brother? Long time no see.

{George} Shucks! You weren't seeing anybody for a few weeks! I'm glad you're alright now, because you gave us all a hell of a scare!

{Brandon} Yeah well, I didn't mean to scare you guys. I thought The Meadows Crew were fearless, what happened!?!

{George} Nothing! Just a little reality set in. I'm going home today, but I will be back to check on you. Are you good? Do you need something?

{Brandon} Nope I will be just fine! Just fine!

True to the Game

{Montego meets with Paul at his office.}

{Montego} Hey Paul what's going on!?!

{Paul} Well Montego I tell you, it's never a dull moment. The crew was attacked yesterday at the Georgia warehouse.

{Montego} What!?! Selena was there with them?

{Paul} Yeah, she was there, and Porshia got shot! How bad off is she only Heavens knows!

{Montego} Oh my GOD! So, what are we going to do about this!?! Do we need to call Elm?

{Paul} No! Not yet! I must find out what's the status of the situation first. I don't want to move fast on this one. Things are getting out of hand. George is coming home from the hospital, and Brandon is out of the coma.

{Montego} So what you mean things are getting out of hand? That's good news Paul, and besides your heavy hitter is well enough to come home from the hospital. And the other is in recovery, but how is Richard doing? Haven't heard anything from him in a while.

{Paul} I know, but he's been taking care of his wife. Because she's dealing with health issues. So, he's going to be on the M.I.A Just for a while through, until his wife gets better.

{Montego} I see! So, what are we going to do about this situation in Georgia!?!

{Paul} As soon as I know what's going on with Porshia, then I'll know what to do about it. Look I need you close by. So, when I move, then we can handle the Georgia situation.

{Montego} Got'cha Paul! No hesitation!

{Kym and Jason are getting things together. So, they can go and meet the crew in Georgia!}

{Jason} Now Kym . . . Are we going to the A.T.L!?!

{Kym} Yes! We got go and meet the crew there. But I haven't heard anything from them.

{Just then Kym's phone rings, and it's Rachel.}

{Kym} Hey Rachel! Me and Jason are on our way to the airport. So, we can get there. How's everything there?

{Rachel} What!?! You don't know what happened!

{Kym} Wha-wha-What happened!?!

{Rachel} Well Porshia been shot, and we just got her here at the hospital!

{Kym} Got Damn! What and how this happened!?! Who you guys were warring against?

{Rachel} Some wannabe gangsters from the Westside, but they got leveled!

{Kym} Alright we're on our way! We'll meet you guys soon! What hospital he's in!?!

{Rachel} The Memorial Hospital downtown Atlanta!

{Kym} We're on the way!

{Richard} Babe we are blessed! My babe is a cancer survivor! Thank GOD!

{Patricia} Hallelujah GOD! Thank You Jesus!

{Richard} Doing like the doctor said, and it paid off, but JESUS Is . . . The Main Doctor!

{Patricia} Yes, HE Is! No one else will do for you, like JESUS will do!

{Richard} Yes! He has the cure, if you believe!

{At the hospital downtown Atlanta. Porshia is in surgery, and the crew is worried about her condition!}

{Samantha} Rachel! Is Kym coming?

{Rachel} Yes Kym and Jason are on the way. I told Shawn to meet them at the airport.

In Route for Georgia

{Lavis} I wonder what Paul is going to do now?

{Rachel} Damn Lavis! You sound like a cop on that question you just asked.

{Lavis} Girl nonsense! The Hell you talking about!?! A cop indeed!

{Rachel} I'm just saying Lavis! Stop taking things so literal! We got more than enough on our plate right now. Porshia in surgery right now with a hole in her side for crying out loud!

{Samantha} Look Rachel! Calm yourself down. Us being at each other's throats, and It's not going to make a bit of difference for the situation at hand!

{Rachel} But you can best believe and bet your bottom dollar. That Paul Meadows will find a way to overcome all the adversities!

{Samantha} You know it! It's just the nature of Paul!

{Lavis} No matter how things seem, he will find something to make it work in his favor!

{Samantha} I know one thang! He better find a way for us to have our vacay getaway! That I know he better do!

{Kym calls Paul to find out what he knows about, what happened to the crew in Georgia.}

{Kym} Come on Paul, answer the phone!

{Paul} Hello Kym! What's going on?

{Kym} I was about to ask you the same thing! Do you know what happened to the crew in Georgia!?!

{Paul} Yes! I'm aware of what's going on with the crew. So, let me guess, you're on the way there now huh?

{Kym} That I am! Me and Jason should be arriving in Atlanta about an hour.

{Paul} Girl that's why I like you. You always on your game. No hesitations, just the job done! Bottom line. Ok, now that you'll be with the crew. I don't have anything to worry about! Hell, do what you gotta do!

{Kym} Will do Paul!

{Kym and Jason are on the way to Georgia, but Holman and Shultz are finding out about what happened as well.}

{DT Holman} Well crew this just came in on fax! There was a shooting incident in Georgia!

{DT Shultz} Really!?! Does it say who was involved?

{DT Holman} No names, but the memo states that shots were fired around a warehouse on the Northside of town. A local gang started shooting. Method of a (187 Drive-By) The occupants inside the warehouse fired back. Ending result of gunning down some of the gang members. So, who that sounds like to you Shultz?

{DT Shultz} What!?! The Meadows Crew?

{DT Holman} Exactly!

{DT Shultz} So let me get this straight! Just because a shooting incident between a local gang, and some occupants in a warehouse squaring off. You automatically believe Paul is behind it, or got something to do with it?

{DT Holman} I can rest assured that Paul Meadows is somewhere in the shadows of it all!

{DT Shultz} Holman! You better be sure!

WALKING THE INVISIBLE LINE

{DT Holman} Shultz I'm more than sure! I'm positive that he's behind this madness!

{DT Shultz} Okay, but I must tell you. This department has leaks in it! There's a few officers that works for Paul. But we don't know who's who! So, you need to watch what you say around here!

{DT Holman} Are you serious Shultz!?!

{DT Shultz} I'm more than serious. I'm right and exact. And that's a fact!

{Back at the hospital; Porshia is out of surgery and is recovering. Kym and Jason arrive thereafter.}

{Kym} Hey guys we're here now! Any word on Porshia's condition!?!

{Samantha} No not yet. We're waiting for the doctor to let us know what's going on!

{The Doctor walks in to tell the crew about Porshia's condition.}

{Doctor} Ok we've been working on Ms. Brown, and she's going to pull through.

{The crew shouts in relief.}

{Samantha} Oh thank you Doc! Thank you and your team! You guys are the best!

{Lavis} For sure! So how is she Doc?

{Doctor} She's fine, apparently, she was hit in the lower right abdomen, but she's strong though.

{Rachel} Thank GOD! She's too stubborn to die!

{Kym} That she is Rachel! Thant she is!

{Paul and Montego make a surprise visit to the hospital and meet up with the crew.}

{Montego} Well hello Meadows Crew!

{Rachel} Montego! What are you doing here? Where's Paul?

{Paul} Right here. Me and Montego had to make a surprise visit and check up on my girl Porshia. Make sure she's ok

{Montego} Now you all know if you see me, you were going to see Paul.

{Samantha} Well anyway! Porshia is going to be fine. She was hit in the lower right-side abdomen. Thank GOD it didn't travel to the kidney. Doctors had been working on her. Surgery was a complete success! Practically it saved her life!

173

A New Rule in Georgia

{Paul} I see I'm going to make it perfectly clear. Whoever was behind this attack will pay dearly!

{Lavis} Don't worry about that Paul! They already been taken care of, literally handled!

{Samantha} Hell, or shall I say, Leveled!

{Lavis} Yeah you can say that!

{Paul} Don't you guys think, for one solitary moment, that's the end of it! No aftermath; nothing! Believe me . . . There will be a follow up behind the first attack! You can bet on that!

{Selena} Paul! There better not be anything! After the crap we just went through!

{Paul} I'm telling you Selena! You better take heed to what I'm saying, at this point; we don't even know what the attack was about!?!

{Kym} That's right! We must find out, who was behind the attack!?!

{Paul} Yes Meadows Crew, find the ones that was responsible. Then let me know. So, we can make them disappear, like Harry Houdini!

{Rachel} Uhm You guys do remember, that this is a hospital. People can hear everything we're saying. So, let's keep it down!

{Paul} I don't give a Damn where we are! When I speak, humph! People listen anyway!

{Lavis} Now Paul, didn't you say some time ago? To keep our conversations Code verb? Don't be all out in the open about our plans of operation.

{Paul} Lavis when I say, I don't give a Damn! Take it literally that I don't! Are there any further questions!?!

{Kym} Well Damn Paul! You talking like you getting ready to take on all of Georgia!?!

{Paul} No that's not the deal, but what I am saying is this No matter what we got to do, we got to engage to get the job done!

{Back at the Vanderbilt Hospital, Brandon is getting his strength back.}
{Brandon} Hey Doc Am I scheduled therapy today?

{Doctor} Yes you do. Therapy is at 1pm this afternoon. We'll take good care you. Have you feeling like a million bucks! Keep in mind that it's a slow process.

{Brandon} That's great Doc! Step by step.

{The Detectives are on edge about the case.}

{DT Holman} Captain Harris look, we've been investigating the Daniels Disappearing Case for quite some time now, and it's been nothing but a dead end everywhere we turn! This is about to become a cold case at hand! Got Dammit!

{Captain Harris} Well I have mentioned to you before that If you and your team, the ones that I allowed you to have on this case I might add! That if you guys are going after Paul Meadows. You need to have your facts straight your ducks in row! Know everything that you are doing, because if not! You would be the one to pay the piper!

{DT Holman} Damn Captain! Who side are you on? I had to ask Shultz the same thing not to long ago! I'm starting to believe that. I'm fighting a losing battle. It's like all of you are working for Paul Meadows and his crew!

{DT Shultz} Hey guys! Sorry, didn't mean to interrupt. Look Holman, when you get finished talking to the Captain. We need to talk! So, you guys carry on.

{DT Holman} Captain! I'm ready to put this case on ice, but that's just how I'm feeling. But hey, I'm not giving up until the case is solved. But as for Paul Meadows is in concern; he may seem like the model citizen. But he's nothing more than a common low down criminal! That has power in all different kinds of places; areas, and even authorities too I might add.

{Captain Harris} Ok Holman look! If you guys can get me some solid proof and evidence. That the Meadows Crew is behind Daniels Disapearance! Then we got something to work with.

{DT Holman} Don't worry Captain! We're on it!

GO HARD, OR GO HOME!

{Now Paul is really going in on his organization, and crew.}

{Paul} Now crew listen up! It's time to turn the heat up on things.

{Kym} How much heat Paul, and how soon!?!

{Paul} How does asap sounds to you! As far as how much is in concern. Well that all depends.

{Samantha} Depends on what!?!

{Paul} How many adversaries; we have to deal with! Do whatever we got to do!

{Lavis} Paul! Don't forget we still have to be incognito. We don't want too much attention to ourselves.

{Paul} You're right Lavis! This is why I need Richard by my side, he kept me calm; cool; and collected.

{Samantha} When is Richard coming back? Maybe you need to call him!

{Paul} Maybe so, but we still need to handle business! Now Porshia's down and I don't know what's going on with George and Brandon. I guess I'll check on Brandon.

{Jason} Kym and I can handle that Paul. You guys do what you gotta do. We'll head back to the Vanderbilt Hospital, and check on Brandon.

{Rachel} Ok.. Me; Lavis; Samantha. We can take care of things in Georgia, and you guys can head back to Nashville.

{Kym} Yes! Since there's no reason for war right now, unless you guys are not to sure about it!

{Rachel} No! We're sure. So, the four of us got it! Plus, you guys got to check on the warehouse. Making sure that the supplies, and production are moving like it's suppose to.

{Paul} Good deal! In the meantime I have to take a trip with Montego, and and probably Richard!

{Lavis} So where you're headed to now Paul!?!

{Paul} Columbia! And not South Carolina either!

{Kym} Alright Paul; see you when you get back!

{Paul} Siennarra!

WALKING THE INVISIBLE LINE

{Richard receives the call from Paul. To see if he's accompanying him and Montego.}

{Richard} Hello!?!

{Paul} Hello Richard!

{Richard} Paul!?! What's going on!?!

{Paul} I have to take a trip, and I was hoping you can accompany me and Montego on this venture.

{Richard} What's the cost of this venture?

{Paul} Nothing! Just being present. We have to go to Columbia

{Richard} Columbia!?! What's out there?

{Paul} More product that I have to purchase! Oh, and by the way! I have your pay.

{Richard} Really! How much is it?

{Paul} $100,000.. That's for you and yours!

{Richard} Damn! That looks real damn good Paul!

{Paul} I have to take care of my crew! Especially my ride or dies. You guys are the reason why we have the success like we do.

{Richard} Ok Paul! I'll accompany you guys on this venture trip! When are leaving?

{Paul} Tomorrow morning. Is that too soon for you?

{Richard} How long are we going to be out there?

{Paul} Two days tops, if that long! Besides, we need to talk about some serious changes. That I'm planning on implimenting for the future, and I really need you Richard!

{Richard} Ok, we'll talk about it! Plus, I need talk to you too as well!

{Paul} Good! We'll see you tomorrow morning! Around 10 will be good. I'll send my car to come pick you up.

{Richard} Alright! See you then.

CHAPTER 17

TIME FOR A NEW TRANSITION

Thinking of a Master Plan

{At this time, Richard talks to his wife. About the sudden trip that Paul wants him to accompany him with.}

{Patricia} Honey! Who was that on the phone?

{Richard} That was Paul, and he wants me to accompany with him on this trip to Columbia.

{Patricia} When is this trip suppose to taking place? How soon!?!

{Richard} Tomorrow morning.

{Patricia} Tomorrow what!?! What do he mean, tomorrow!

{Richard} Yeah, and he's sending a car to pick me up around 10am.

{Patricia} Now let me get this straight. Paul expects for you! To be ready at the drop of a hat! To go to some, uncharted land? Where man don't give a Damn! And I know Paul don't!

{Richard} Well bae, it's all business! Plus..

{Patricia} Plus it's all, Paul's business! What!?! He don't have enough people and playas to accompany him with!?!

{Richard} Yes dear, but he only trust me for this venture! Besides he has my money, or shall I say our money.

{Patricia} What kind of money he's talking about? A few thousands!?!

{Richard} How about a hundred thousand to be exact! Now what you got say babe?

{Patricia} A hundred thousand dollars!?!

{Richard} Yes! Plus we need to have a talk about the upcoming, or shall I say; the inevitable! About this business. I believe Paul is going to leave for a little while.

{Patricia} If that is true. Then, who's going to take over while he's gone?

{Richard} Babe, you already know who he wants to take over. On his leave of absence.

{Patricia} I was afraid of that. Besides, what do you know about what Paul do in his business!?!

{Richard} I know enough to get us by, and what I don't know, Kym could show me.

{Patricia} Now look here! If you think, that I'm gonna sit here, and just allow my husband to leave without knowing the full detail of what this is all about! Huh! Think again Yogi, Because Boo boo's coming with you!

{Richard} Aww come on babe!

{Patricia} Now that's final babe! So, what time Paul's car is scheduled to arrive!?! Oh I'm not taking no for an answer. Oh by the way, how many days are we staying?

{Wow Patricia is something else, but George is anxious to get back into the swing of things!}

{George} Man! I got to call either Paul, or Kym. Or somebody in the crew. To let me know what's up!

{George calls Paul to find out what's next!}

{Paul} Hello? Oh hey George, and how are you doing? I guess you're calling to find out what's going on!?!

{George} You know it Paul! So, when can I get back to work? I might've been shot, but I can still pistol pack in the back!

{Paul} I know George, but I can use you with the crew Because I got to take a leave of absence.

{George} So, where you going Paul?

{Paul} I can't tell over the phone. I will let Kym fill you in on the details about everything that you'll need to know.

{George} So, how soon you want me to get with the crew?

{Paul} Don't worry, Kym will contact you soon enough! In the meantime I need for you to keep a check on Brandon, and you to be getting your strength back.

{George} No doubt Paul! No doubt.

THINGS ARE GETTING MESSY, TIME TO LAY LOW

{Paul calls for a meeting with everyone. Before he leaves.}

{Paul} Montego call Kym; Rachel; George and let them know that I have to meet with everyone before we go. I'm sending the car for Richard. He'll be joining us on our trip.

{Montego} Paul why meet with the crew before we leave? We're only going for a couple of days.

{Paul} I know, but those Detectives are on my case. So we got lay low. That's the real reason why I must go. Plus I have something in store for Detective Holman.

{Montego} Aww man! What you got in mind for him? Damn, don't keep me in the dark! So, what's the measure Paul?

{Paul} Well thanks to my pocket paid informants. I can stay on top of any raids; infertraition. Anything the cops want to intervene with my business! But like I said I got something for Detective Holman!

That's going to blow his mind! Also to let him know, don't mess with Paul Meadows!

{Montego} I heard that! Haha! Poor Holman.

{Rachel} Hello? Oh Hi Montego! What's going on!?!

{Montego} Paul wants to meet with everyone before our departure. Let Kym know the 411 as well with the others.

{Rachel} Ok, I will inform the others.

{Kym} Rachel, what's happening with Paul?

{Rachel} Paul wants to meet with the crew before they leave the country, like asap!

{Kym} Hello!?! George how are you?

{George} I'm good! Paul wants me to get with you guys before he leaves!

{Kym} Ok Shawn will have to come get you. So we can meet in a timely fashion. I'm sending him now. Look we'll get to you!

{George} Good looking out Kym! See y'all when you get here.

{Now the crew has assembled together. Now Paul can let the crew know what's the next phase in operation.}

{Paul} Montego, now you can contact Elm! I'm gonna need him to handle something for me once and for all!

{Montego} No problem Paul. Consider it a done deal!

{Paul} No! I want a Disappearing Act!

{Montego} Oh okay! The magician has to perform his magic . . . Abracadabra! Allah Disappearo, Poof be gone!

{Just then Richard and Patricia walks in the meeting room.}

{Richard} Well well well! Paul and Montego, are y'all ready for this trip or not!?!

{Paul} Damn straight we're ready for the trip.

{Montego} What's good with you Richard!?! Oh and I see the Mrs is joined along with you.

{Patricia} Yes! I certainly did Montego!

{Paul} Hey Rich, can I speak to you for a minute, uhmm excuse us won't you Patricia!?!

{Richard} What's going on Paul?

{Paul} Now Richard, you already know the deal! It's not safe for Patricia to accompany us on our voyages.

{Richard} I know Paul, I know! But I tried to keep her at home, but this time she literally insisted that she's coming on this trip. So, what the hell am I supposed to do?

{Paul} Man! Do what you gotta do! To make sure your family stay safe! Now, how does this reflect on you. For me to entrust that you can handle business for me when I'm gone!?!

{Richard} Look Paul, I got this alright! I can take care of any and everything that I need to! My wife, I can handle her, but keep in mind Paul. That she's use to me being by her side. So, I have to get her use to me leaving from time to time.

{Paul} Ok! Being that we're omly going for a couple of days. I will allow for her to come this time. But don't let it become habitual!

{Richard} Okay Paul, I understand.

No Time to Lose

{Now the crew meets Paul, and Montego before the departure.}

{Kym} Hey Paul, we're all here now. Now usually you'll already be gone. So, why are we meeting up before you go! This is odd.

{Paul} The reason I called for this meeting is because, I'm going to take a leave of absence. So, you guys have to keep the business afloat.

{Rachel} We got you Paul! But what about the products in the Tri State Area? Also Maryland; Georgia; Florida, and Texas!?!

{Samantha} Don't worry Rachel, we can handle it! Even if we all have to go together to each and every one of those states. To make sure, that everything is going accordingly as planned.

{Lavis} Yeah! Don't worry Paul, we'll take care of everything. Just leave it to us.

{Paul} I know I can count on you guys, but the main reason I called this meeting is. Someone is getting ready to disappear.

{The crew replied Who's that going to be!?!}

{Paul} That Damn Holman, but it's not going to be easy to take him out!

{Kym} Yes he needs to go! But you're right Paul. It's not going to be easy to get him.

{Lavis} So, how you plan to eliminating him?

{Samantha} That's going to be tedious! Taking out a cop! Now you're asking for trouble.

{Montego} Yes, but it's not impossible. Cause he can still get got!

{Richard} Hey Paul! You ready?

{Paul} Oh yeah! I'm ready, but look y'all I want him gone! I'm sick and tired of Detective Holman. Popping up every time I turn around there he is!?!

{Richard} Hey Paul, it's time to go! We have a flight to catch.

{Lavis} Richard! You going too!?!

{Richard} Oh yeah! I'm going to make sure Paul and Montego gets to the airport!

{Kym} Wow! For a minute there I thought you were going too.

{Samantha} That's what it sounded like!

{Paul} Well it wasn't! But if I were to decide for Richard to go with me. It would be my perrogative. Wouldn't it?

{Paul} Alright y'all! You know what I expect. So handle the business as accordingly.

{Kym} You got it Paul.

{Paul; Montego; Richard and Patricia leaves the crew to go to the airport. They talked amongst themselves in the car on the way. Just then a dark colored sedan rolls up alongside their vehicle.}

{Montego} Hey uhmm Paul, or Richard. Do anyone knows this vehicle coming alongside our car!?!

{Paul} No I don't!

{Just then shots rang out! Striking their vehicle! Richard hits the gas hard, and races out of there!}

{Montego} Who the hell are these guys!?!

{Paul} I don't know! But they gonna find out who we are! Montego you strapped?

{Montego} Yep!

{Paul} Well so am I!

{Paul and Montego returns fire to the sedan. Both vehicles driving erratically down the street.}

{Richard} What the Hell man!?! Who are these cats?

{Montego} Drive Richard! We'll take care of these bastards! Paul, shoot the front left tire!

{Paul} Ha! You must've been reading my mind!

{Paul shoots out their front left tire, and kaboom! The sedan flips forward several times.}

{Montego} Yeah! Now that's how you handle perpetrators. Alright Richard smooth it out!

{Richard} Yeah Montego! Hey honey you ok!?! Patricia honey you can relax now babe. Patricia!?! Oh my GOD! She's not responding!

{Paul} Patricia! Richard! She's been hit!

{Richard} What!?! What the Hell! Patricia bae!

{Montego} Look man we gotta get her to the hospital! Now like pronto! Go man! Just go!

AN INTERRUPTED VOYAGE

{As Richard speeding down the street. Paul is trying to keep Patricia comfortable as possible.}

{Paul} Richard! How far are we from the hospital!?! She's bleeding heavily!

{Montego} We only have a couple of towels!

{Richard} Bae! Bae! Stay with us! Is she aware Paul? What si she doing!?!

{Paul} Losing alot of blood! Oh good we're near the hospital!

{George} Doggone; I wonder where Paul, Montego and Richard are right about now?

{Samantha} Well they should be arriving at the airport shortly.

{George} Ohh yeah I almost forgot! Brandon is doing much better.

{The crew replied in harmony! That's great! Yeah! We knew Brandon would be alright!}

{Kym} Well you guys, let's get back to work! We got alot to take care of!

{Lavis} True that, but how are we going to take care of those Detectives?

{Rachel} I'm not sure yet, but we will somehow!

{Just then Montego calls Kym, and tells the disturbing news.}

{Montego} Kym! Kym! Listen up, Patricia just got shot! As we were on the to the airport.

{Kym} Oh my GOD! What the Hell happened!

{Montego} Look! The four of us were riding down the street. On the way to the airport. When a black car rode alongside our car. Next thing we knew, shots rang out! Richard hauls ass out of there as fast as he could, but they were on our tail!

{Kym} So where are you guys now!?!

{Montego} At the hospital downtown!

{Kym} Now why was Patricia with you guys!?! She had no business there with y'all!

{Lavis} Kym! What's going on!?!

{Kym} Paul; Montego; Richard was involved in a rolling shoot out, and Patricia got shot! They're at the hospital downtown. We got to there now! Let's move people!

{Now the police is at the scene where the sedan crashed. The two males in the vehicle. Dead!}

{Officer Peele} Damn Shultz! I wonder what hell happened to these guys?

{DT Shultz} Wow! Hell is right, and according to witnesses. They were traveling southbound chasing another vehicle. Shooting at each other. Until the other shot out the front left tire. In results sends the sedan on a triple F!

{Officer Peele} Triple F!?!

{DT Schultz} A Flight Flipping Forward!

{DT Holman} Alrighty then! What do we have here? Two dead in a turned over sedan. Along with enough fire power to start a war. We got to investigate this crime scene.

{DT Shultz} And what a crime scene it is!?!

{Meanwhile at the hospital, the doctors are working on Patricia, and Richard is in a uproar!}

{Richard} I knew I should've never let her come with us! It's all my fault! If I only said no!

{Paul} Look Richard, it's not your fault! We have to keep in mind! We have to keep family and business separate.

{Richard} I just don't know why she wanted to come!?! If my baby only would've stayed at home. She wouldn't have gotten shot!

{Montego} Look Rich my man, we got to stay positive. She gonna be just fine.

{At that point the crew walks in, and the doctor walks in simultaneously!}

{Richard} Hey Doc, what's happening!?! How's my wife?

{Doctor} Are you Mr. Miles?

{Richard} Yes! Yes I am Doc, what's going on with my wife!?!

{The Doctor looks at Richard, but hesitant to answer.}

{Doctor} Uhmm Mr. Miles can I speak to you in private?

No Relief for the Closer.

{Richard looks at the doctor as if his heart had stopped!}

{Richard} Doc, what's going on!?! How is my wife? I gotta go in and see her!

{Doctor} Hold on! Hold on! Mr. Miles.

{Richard} Doc it ain't no holding on! I got to go in there, she's in there waiting on me! Move y'all! Move!

{Doctor} Mr. Miles you can't go in there!

{Richard} Why the hell not!?!

{Doctor} She's gone!

{Paul; Richard, and Montego all looked at the doctor in zombie like stares.}

{Richard} What!?! What did you say Doc?

{Doctor} We worked as vigorously as we could, but she didn't pull through. I'm so sorry! A bullet had peirced through the heart, and to the right lung. We revived her twice, but on the third time; she slipped away. She didn't come back. I'm so sorry Mr. Miles.

{The crew walks in, but now with disbelief on their faces when they heard the news.}

{Richard} Nooo! Not my Patricia! Hell no!}

{The crew is trying to console Richard. In hope of getting him to calm down.}

{Lavis} Rich man! Rich! Calm down my brother!

{Paul} Look everybody, let Rich get it all out! Your not going to be able to console him right now!

{Samantha} We got to help him! Can't just let Rich go buck wild up in here!

{Paul} Trust me Sam, let hm be, but keep him on monitor! So he won't hurt someone, or himself! Understood!?!

{Samantha} Well understood Paul!

{George} Richard tell us man, what happened?

{Montego} I tell you. We was riding to the airport. When a couple of guys in a dark sedan rolls up on the side of us, and started shooting at our car!

Richard punches the gas. Next thing we knew . . . Were in a high speed chase shootout! Paul shoots out their front tire. Their car flips forward, but Patricia got hit in the process! We made it here, but she didn't make it!

{After leaving the scene. The detectives are on their way to the hospital. In hopes to find answers to the crime based scenario!}

{DT Holman} We going to find the answers to this crime scenario.

{DT Shultz} Where at Holman?

{DT Holman} At the hospital! I wonder, I really wonder! Of how, or why this transpired.

{DT Shultz} Well the bodies of the two in the black sedan are on their way to the morgue. So what would be the connection at the hospital.

{DT Holman} You see Shultz . . . Anybody that was involved with that race and chase shootout! You better believe, someone went to the hospital.

{Officer Peele} Well what are we waiting for? Let's go to the hospital.

{George} Paul! Now you know the police is going to be here momentarily! I'm surprised they didn't beat us here! So what are you going to do now?

{Paul} Montego and I still gotta go. Even more so, because Holman will be investigating the shooting incident. And you know I'm public enemy #1!

{Montego} You know this Paul. So we need to go before they get here.

{Richard} Look I'm going to be ok! So Paul and Montego you guys go ahead without me. I have alot to tend to. My baby is gone. I'm in a twilight zone right now.

{Paul} Look Rich, If you need anything! Don't hesitate to contact me. I got you bro!

{Richard} Yeah, thanks Paul!

{The crew consoles Richard, but by this time the police are pulling up at the hospital!}

CHAPTER
18

A Trip to the Badlands

Don't Come, Unless We Send 4 Ya!

{As the police pulled up outside the hospital, Paul and Montego are leaving out of the door.}

{Paul} Well hello Detectives Holman and Shultz. Lovely day in the neighbor huh!?!

{DT Holman} Paul! Let me ask you a question, and I'm gonna get straight to the point. Do you know anything about a couple of cars chasing and shooting at one another!?!

{Paul} Well no officer Holman, Oh I'm sorry Detective . . . Holman.

{DT Holman} Don't get smart with me Paul! I have a feeling that you do know about it!

{Montego} No he don't Holman! You know, if you would actually do some got damn police work, and stop harrassing innocent people! You just might catch some bad guys for a change!

{DT Holman} Boy! You guys always got something smart to say out of your mouths! I know it's not going to be long before you guys make that fatal mistake.

{Paul} You know what, your right Holman! We are going to make that fatal mistake, but it will be on purpose though!

{DT Shultz} What do you mean by that Mr. Meadows!?!

Paul} Nothing much, just suggesting; or shall I say i'm in agreement with you, Detective Holman. But for now Goodbye! Oh and another thing. Don't come for us; unless we send for ya! Okay!

{DT Holman} Huh! Don't worry about that Paul, we'll come regardless!

{The Detectives entered the lobby for a briefing with the nurse. To find out if anyone came in with connections about the accident.}

{Nurse} Hello, and how may I help you?

{DT Shultz} Yes Detectives Shultz and Holman. We're looking to see if anyone came in that was involved in an accident possibly within the past 30 minutes or so.

{Nurse} Well my shift just started, so I'm not sure what's going on; but I will look into it!

{DT Shultz} Thank you so much we greatly appreciate it.

{Nurse} No problem at all Detective.

Walking the Invisible Line

{Richard} I hope those detectives don't come in here to ask us any questions!

{Kym} Don't you worry about them Rich, we'll stop them right in their tracks.

{Lavis} That's right Richard! You just worry about what you're going to do next.

{Richard} I don't know what I'm going to do next man. I feel like I'm in a twilight zone! My wife, the love of my life is gone! For something that she had nothing to do with.

{Rachel} You guys done handled the fools that shot at y'all!

{Richard} Yeah! Paul and Montego done put a stop to those guys once, and for all!

{Lavis} Now you already know the police will be investigating. So what are you going to tell them!?! Cause you know their coming to find out if anyone else was involved.

{Kym} Well they don't have anything to convict you with. So you don't have anything to worry about.

{Richard} Maybe not, but I don't want them asking me nothing! Don't even look my way.

{No sooner than Richard just getting the words out of his mouth. Here comes Detectives Holman and Shultz.}

{DT Holman} Well hello Meadows Crew, and how you guys doing on a day like today!?! Good day for a killing huh?

{Just then Richard lunges into Holman. It caught everybody by surprise!}

{Richard} Holman, if you and your partner don't get your asses out of here! I swear you gonna wish you had!

{DT Holman} Richard! I don't know what's going on right now, but I will find out everything in full detail. But I can assure you, if you ever come at me like that again, and you will regret it for a long damn time! Just try me if you think I'm bluffing!

Be Careful for What you Ask 4

{Paul} Hey Montego, did you get a load of the BS that Holman trying to shovel out!?!

{Montego} Yeah! I don't know what he was trying to prove, but he better back up. He better recognize who the hell he's dealing with!

{Meanwhile back in the Vanderbilt Hospital, Brandon's going home.}

{Brandon} Thank you Doc! For all your help! Yes I am finally going home!

{Doctor} Yes today is the day that you're out of here! We can schedule you an appointment for next week, to continue your physical therapy.

{Brandon} Ok Doc! I can come in for the therapy, but I have to get back to my stores.

{Doctor} I understand that you want to get back to work as soon as possible. Just keep it very simple, and don't try to do much. No heavy lifting, no stressful movements. You know; take it slow and easy! Until you heal properly.

{Brandon} Ok I understand doctor!

{Doctor} Good deal.

{Porshia} Oh my GOD! What happened to me!?!

{Doctor} You just came out of surgery, not to long ago. A lot has happened since you been gone. Hey, welcome back!

{Porshia} Gone! What do you mean, gone?

{Doctor} You've been shot, but you're doing fine now. Thank GOD! We thought you were gone for good.

{Porshia} I wonder if the crew is here?

{Doctor} Yes! Some of them are still here.

{Porshia} Can they come in Doctor?

{Doctor} Sure they can.

{Paul} You know what Montego, I've been thinking about all the attacks my crew has been going through, and I believe that someone is really trying to take me and my crew out!

{Montego} You know what Paul, you may need to hire spies. To find out who's behind all the attacks.

{Paul} Don't you think that I have more than enough people to find out for me!

{Montego} Nope, and I say this because; everyone that works for you is known. Now you hire a spy, they're incognito. No one would suspect they work for you.

{Paul} Well that sounds like a plan that I need to put into operation.

{Back at the hospital, detectives Holman and Shultz are looking for answers behind the shooting incident.}

{DT Holman} Now Shultz, I truly feel that Paul Meadows is behind all of kaos that's been going on around here, and other places as well.

{DT Shultz} Now Holman, we got a lot going on right now, and all of this is linked to Paul Meadows and his crew! You really got it in for him huh!?!

{DT Holman} Because he's the only one, who's capable of doing all of these things! The only explanation, but you know what Shultz. He's not the only one who's gangster around here!

{DT Shultz} Holman, what the hell are you talking about?

{DT Holman} Well what I'm talking about is this! It takes gangster; to take down a gangster!

{DT Shultz} Haha! What other gangster? Is taking down Paul Meadows and his crew!?!

{DT Holman} Oh I'll be that one to do so!

{DT Shultz} First off Holman, you don't know the first thing about taking down a gangster! Let alone being one! So how could you. Take down the most Notorious Mobster Paul Meadows!?!

TIGHTER THE VICE; THE TIGHTER THE GRIP!

{DT Holman} You see Shultz, I've been knocking on the Meadows Crew door for quite some time now, and believe me when I tell you They're not too hard to knock down!

{DT Shultz} Believe me when I tell you Holman, again that I might add. When you're going after Paul and his crew! You better know what you're doing! But you going to see, and I hope you don't have to learn the hard way!

{DT Holman} Don't worry, we got this!

{Brandon calls George. To see how he's doing.}

{George} Hello, hey what's going on Brandon!?! Man it's been a while! So how you feeling?

{Brandon} I'm okay bro! I'm sorry I couldn't be with you guys, but I got to check on my stores as soon as possible!

{George} Well damn man you can't just come out the hospital, and expect to start work right away! You need your rest.

{Brandon} Rest! Man later for rest, I got businesses to run and maintain!

{George} Man Brandon I feel you! Your mind is telling you one thing, and your body is telling you something else. So I think, you better listen to your body.

{Brandon} Yeah I guess you're right! Even though I still want to check on my stores!

{George} Look the crew is here, and we can't wait to all get together and handle business.

{Brandon} Same here bro!

{Richard} What am I going to do now!?! My baby is gone! I wish you were here Patricia. I really miss you! Damn bastards took my wife's life!

{Richard recieves a calls from Paul!}

{Paul} Hey Richard! I'm just calling to check on you, and see if you're alright.

Walking the Invisible Line

{DT Holman} You see Shultz, Paul Meadows might be a powerful mogul in the state of Tennessee, but we can bring him, and his crew down. It will take alot of effort! But it's not impossible.

{DT Shultz} Now we've been working on this Missing Persons Case for months, and everywhere we turned it's been nothing but a Paul Meadows headache!

{DT Holman} Well like I said Shultz, it takes a gangster; to bring down a gangster!

{DT Shultz} Just like Mounds and Almond Joy said, Sometimes you feel like a nut! And sometimes you don't!

{DT Holman} Haha! Very funny! But I'm serious about that Shultz. The thing about it is. Paul will never suspect or even knew what hit him, until it's too late.

{DT Shultz} What the hell are you talking about Holman!?!

{DT Holman} For starters do you remember the incident where two of Paul's crew members got shot!?!

{DT Shultz} You talking about George and Brandon. That took place outside of Brandon's Meat Market?

{DT Holman} Yep! That's the one!

{DT Shultz} What did you do Holman!?!

{DT Holman} Let's just say I too have connections in high and low places may I add!

{DT Shultz} I don't get it! I thought it was a local group that ambushed those two?

{DT Holman} It was! But some friends of mine helped me out. To setup the ambush. Haha!

{DT Shultz} Who? You can tell me. Who was it!

{DT Holman} Benjamin, and Jackson! You know they don't play no favors!

{DT Shultz} You Son of a Bitch! You paid some local gang bangers to take out George and Brandon!?!

{DT Holman} Not only money talks, but it certainly controls the weak in minded! And there's more from where that came from! That's just the tip of the iceberg! I got more in store for Mr. Meadows and His Crew, and you can take that to the bank!

TWISTED AS WE GO, HUH!?!

{Paul and Montego leaves for the airport, but not Columbia! Instead, they're heading for New York.}

{Mantego} Ok Paul, now we're heading for Columbia Huh!?!

{Paul} No Not right now! It's too much going on for me to take a leave of absence. Even if it's still about business. My colleagues at the office has new building projects that's ready for inspection. So I have to take care of other things first! Remember, business before pleasure!

{Montego} Alright, but what about the others!?!

{Paul} My crew is tight, but they been under attack lately.

{Montego} Lately!?! That's using the term loosely. More than lately is more like it!

{Kym calls Jason for a meet with him at the warehouse.}

{Jason} Hello Kym, and what may I have the honor of doing for you!?!

{Kym} I'm good Jay! I have to meet with you at the warehouse. To go over the books, and the crew is coming also.

{Jason} Ok sounds good. Maybe we can get to the bottom of all the attacks that's been going on.

{Kym} Yes we're going to be discussion about these issues that the crew has been facing.

{Jason} Well then, I see you guys when y'all get here! Oh yeah, bring some food too. I already have the drinks.

{Richard's at home trying to gather his thoughts on what he's going to do next.}

{Richard} Gotta call my in-laws, and tell them about Patricia. Let them know about the funeral arrangements.

{Richard makes calls to the family, but just as he was making his final call. Shots were fired at his front door!}

{Richard} What the Hell is going on here!?!

{Richard takes cover as he crawls to where he keeps his guns! He takes a glance out the window, and creeps out the back door. He starts firing back at the perpetrators out front. Until they sped off in their vehicles.}

{Rachel calls Richard to see how he's doing.}

{Richard} Hey Rachel, what's going on!?!

{Rachel} Nothing much. I just wanted to call and see how you were doing. You ok, do you need anything? If you do we got your back!

{Richard} Yeah well, I'm gonna need you guys to come to my place!

{Rachel} Why what's wrong!?!

{Richard} Some fools shot up the front part of my house! How soon can you guys get over here! Plus I got to call the police.

{Rachel} Got Dammit! We're on our way!

{Back at police station, Detectives Holman and Shultz are rounding up the squad for a raid!}

{Officer Peele} Hey Holman! Just in from 911, a shooting incident occured at a local residential home, and it seems to be at a familiar address.

{DT Holman} What's the address?

{Officer Peele} 521 Slate Drive.

{DT Shultz} Ain't that the Miles address? Richard Miles?

{DT Holman} Why yes it is as a matter of fact! Wow! It's funny how things just happen. When you least expected. Well let's go see if Mr Miles is fine!

{DT Shultz} Hey Holman! You wouldn't have anything to do with this incident. Would you?

{DT Holman} Shultz! When you're living that kind of lifestyle, you need to expect, the unexpected! Now for Paul and his crew, huh deal with it! And now here comes one time!

Walking the Invisible Line Deal With Whatever Comes Your Way

{Kym; George; Lavis, and Samantha, meets Jason at the warehouse. Not aware of what happened at Richard's house.}

{Jason} Hey gang what's going on?

{Kym} Everything! That's not is going on.

{George} It seem strange that, everything was going great. Until those detectives started snooping around the warehouse. That's when things started going haywire!

{Kym} You know what George? You're right! You are absolutely right! That's when things started going crazy for the crew.

{Lavis} So you guys thinking what I'm thinking!?! That Holman and his compadres, had something to do with all the unfortunate mishaps. We been dealing with!?!

{Samantha} I wouldn't be surprised! Crooked Ass Cops will do anything to make they're mark.

{At that moment Kym receives a call from Rachel!}

{Kym} What's up Rachel!?!

{Rachel} Look! Richard house has been shot up!

{Kym} What!?!

{Rachel} Yes girl! He called me and told me that some guys shot up his house, but he's ok though.

{Kym} Oh Thank GOD! So what do he want to do? Do he want to call the police, or shall we roll through!?!

{Rachel} I believe he called the police, but he still wants to handle this situation himself.

{Kym} Ok I guess that means we're rolling through huh!?!

{Rachel} I can assure you on that, we're definitely rolling through!

{Richard calls Paul.}

{Paul} Hello, hey what's going Richard?

{Richard} Some guys came by here, and shot up my house man!

{Paul} What! Are you alright!?!

{Richard} Yeah I'm good, but the front of my house isn't! Riddled up with bullet holes.

{Paul} Did you get a look at the guys, or were they in disguise?

{Richard} Three of them! All dressed in black. They move like ratfinks that shot at us, and killed my wife! I swear man, if they are afiliated with the same ones!?! They got Hell to pay also!

{Paul} I really believe that someone is trying to get under my skin! I'm going to find out who's behind all the attacks!

{Richard} Don't worry about that Paul! We will see who's behind it all!

{The crew is going to meet at Richard's house, and discuss how to get back at the ones who shot up Richard's house!}

{Kym} Let's go so we can check on Richard, and make sure he's ok!

{Samantha} What about Porshia and Brandon? Porshia's still down, and Brandon's is out of the hospital. Doing GOD knows what!

{Lavis} More than likely, checking out his stores!

{Brandon walks in on the conversation, and states.}

{Brandon} Or.. Brandon could be here with his crew, and going to make sure Richard is good!

{Rachel} Well alright! Let's move people!

{Kym} Oh by the way! Is everyone strapped?

{The crew replied, Hell yeah!}

CHAPTER 19

SHOUTING FOR THE SHOWDOWN

REVENGE IS A DISH, BEST SERVED COLD!

{Paul and Montego are contemplating on what to do about the attacks!}

{Montego} Ok Paul, what are we going to do about the situation dealing with Richard?

{Paul} I know Montego, and believe me! There will be no stone unturned! Wait a minute Montego! I got a call.

{Paul receives a call from an allied, to inform him about the attacks!}

{Informant} Alright Paul! The attacks had been contemplated by The Southsiderz; and also Detective Holman!

{Paul} Oh really now! Thank you for the Information. I'll take of it!

{Montego} Hey Paul . . . Who was that on phone?

{Paul} My informant has told me the ones behind the attacks! First of all those Southsiderz from Baltimore, and my arch enemy.

{Montego} What!?! Are you sure!

{Paul} With 100% accurracy! So you know what's gonna happen right?

{Montego} Yes! It's time for Houdini to perform another disappearing act! Now who's going in the box first!?! Who's the first contestant?

{Paul} I'm going to deal with the Southsiderz first; then I got something special in store for those detectives. As a matter of fact! I got something to show for all to see, and my crew; you and I will be present for this!

{Montego} Oh really Paul? It's going to be worth for all of us to be there?

{Paul} Yes! I wouldn't have it any other way. But not yet! We got to go and take the trip to New York.

{Montego} I thought we were going to Columbia!?!

{Paul} Yeah that's what I wanted everybody to believe. So I won't be trailed there. You can't let the right hand know what the left hand is doing!

{Montego} Well I'm glad you didn't leave me in the dark. So what are we going to do about Richard's situation?

{Paul} Don't worry about that! My crew is going to handle the situation.

{Meanwhile the Meadows Crew is gearing up for the payback!}

{Kym} Lavis! Call George, and tell him to meet us at the airport.

{Lavis} Sure thing, but what's going on Kym?

{Kym} It's time to lay some heads to bed!

{Lavis} The ones who attacked Richard's home! Oh Hell yeah!

{Lavis calls George to let him know to meet the crew at the airport, and definitely strap up!}

{Lavis} What's good George! Look we got to meet up at the airport.

{George} Yo! What's going on Lavis!?! Anything wrong?

{Lavis} Right now! We can't talk about that! Just get there! Oh yeah . . . It's time for some Miami Heat to come blazing! You feel me!?!

{George} Roger, Loud and clear! See you guys at the airport, and I'll be ready for action too!

{Lavis} Alright he's meeting us there. Now what!?!

{Kym} Samantha; Rachel; Lavis; and George. Have the guns ready! Because it's payback time. Paul done found out who's responsible for all the attacks.

{Samantha} What! Who was it!?!

{Kym} The Southsiderz in Baltimore, and Detective Holman!

{Rachel} Wait a minute! How can that be? When the so called leader of the Southsiderz is part of the foundation of Paul's newly contracted building!?!

{Kym} Well apparently, Detective Holman paid off the Southsiderz to do some dirty work for him! Also he's been playing gangster himself.

{Lavis} Wow! So Holman is Gangster huh!?! Maybe it's time for a showdown then!

{Kym} No Lavis! Not right now! Paul told me to hold off from him for now! He said he got something in store for DT Wannabe Gangster Holman! You know Paul got insiders on the force.

PAYBACK'S A BITCH! AIN'T IT!?!

{The crew met at the airport. Now it's time make shit happen!}

{George} What's good Meadows Crew!?!

{Kym} Time for some disappearing act. You ready!?!

{George} Damn straight Kym! Who's first to take out on the menu?

{Kym} First; The Westside crew in Miami! They were the ones that attacked us in Florida.

{George} I thought you guys leveled them already?

{Kym} Not all them! Come to find out by Paul's informant. They attacked Paul; Montego; Richard and killed his wife. They're connected with the Southsiderz from Baltimore.

{George} Really! Ok let's go lay these fools down! Shawn! Ready to take flight!?!

{Shawn} Ready when you are!

{Samantha} Hey let's do this!

{The Meadows Crew strapped and loading up on the jet. Ready; Set; Go!}

{Montego} Paul what the crew is up to?

{Paul} Right now their on the way to Miami. To take care of the first set of violaters. The Westside crew in Miami, Florida. There they will get further instructions for what's next. Or shall I say,"Who's next on the Menu of Death!

{Montego and Paul laughs about the situation, but on the other part of town. Detectives Holman and Shultz are brewing up their own scheme, to takedown Paul and His Crew!}

{DT Holman} You see Shultz! Paul is not the only one who's gangster around here.

{DT Shultz} Yeah, but you know it's going to come to a point for a showdown! Between us and them.

{DT Holman} So what bring it babe! I'm tired of all the BS! Playing tit for tat! What some; come and get some!

{DT Shultz} You know what Holman! You're playing a dangerous game with them. You need to chill the hell out! I've been warning you for so long about Paul Meadows! But you'll learn about him.

{The crew is about to land in Miami. Mission 1, The Westside Crew Elimination!}
{George} Alright! Where they at?
{Kym} We can't be so obvious! So play it cool George. Don't worry we'll get them all this time.
{Samantha} What about Miami Heat?
{Kym} What about them!?! By the time we do what got do . . . They'll just be notified, and we'll be gone!
{Lavis} That's right! Our connections will link us to they're hangout spot.
{Rachel} Well what the Hell are we waiting for? Call'em up Lavis! It's time for a Smackdown, Permanate Takedown!
{Lavis makes a call to Elm! He lets Lavis know they're whereabouts. Brandon calls Paul for the latest news.}
{Brandon} Hey Paul, what's good with you and the crew?
{Paul} Brandon! What a surprise to hear from you! Well the crew is in Miami. To take care of some business for me.
{Brandon} Really! What happening in the Sunshine State!?!
{Paul} No discussion over the phone! Are you up to participating in the crew's activities!?!
{Brandon} I thought you'd never ask, Hell yeah I'm up for some participating in crew fun! I always keep my cutters sharp and jagged. As a matter of fact. I'm on my way, get Shawn on the horn; and I'll be waiting at the airport in an hour!
{Paul} Bet! I'll have him there asap!
{Now the Crew has been looking for the remaining members of the Westside Crew.}
{Shawn recieves a call from Paul.}
{Shawn} Hey what's up Paul!?! Everything's good with you?
{Paul} Sure, but I need you to fly back to pick up Brandon at the airport.
{Shawn} Uh Oh! I know what that means . . . He's Back!

{Paul} Damn straight! Brandon's been missing out of the Meadows Crew Games! It's very sporting of him to participate once again.
{Shawn} I'm on my way, Three hours tops! So, tell Brandon hang tight. I'll be there.

Take them Out; One by One!

{As the Meadows Crew headed towards the warehouse to check on the merchandise and product. One of the Westside crew members was spotted by Rachel.}

{Rachel} Lavis! Isn't that one of those Westsiders across the street?

{Lavis} Damn right it is! Let's get'em!

{Kym} What's going on!?!

{Rachel} Westsider across the street!

{The Westsider spotted The Meadows Crew, and ran like his life depend on it. The Meadows gave chase, and surrounded the individual. George pulls his gun out, and put the gun to the guy's temple.

{Westsider Markus} Look here, I ain't nothing to do with the ambush the Westside Crew did to you guys!

{George} Dammit! If you didn't have anything to do with the ambush, then how you know it was a ambush? Bitch! You lying your ass off!

{Kym} Your Markus aren't you!?!

{Markus} Yeah! What's it to you? Slant eyes!?!

{Kym} Oh! Smart Ass Huh!?! George . . . Light his ass up! Oh yeah, Markus Goodnight!

{Two shots from George's gun was all that you heard. The crew took his limp body in the alleyway. Covered up the body with linen from the dumpster. Lavis went into the store to purchase plenty of lighter fluid. The crew threw Markus body in the dumpster. Drenched with the lighter fluid, and lit a match. Tossed it in the dumpster, now it's an enclosed furnace; hell like a fireplace.}

Walking the Invisible Line

{Samantha} Light'em up! Light'em up! Flame on! Watch him burn till the smoke is gone!?!

{Kym} No thanks! Dead is good enough for me! Remember Meadows . . . No proof or evidence of The Meadows Crew dirty work.

{Rachel} Now this is how we going to get away with it. Frame Markus for snitching on his own crew!

{George} Now you know the Westsiders ain't going to believe that.

{Rachel} Yes they will! Get the word to them that Markus was planning to set them up! So we wouldn't come after him.

{George} Then they would want to war with us!

{Kym} No matter, we want they're asses anyway! So we gonna make them an offer that they will not refuse!

{Lavis} And if they don't agree to our terms?

{Rachel} Then they're asses are going to take permanent dirt naps! Simple, and that's that!

{George} Ok! But personnally . . . I rather find their hideout. Lace some C4 around them, and kaboom!

{Kym} I feel you George, but we're getting a little beside ourselves. Remember incognito Meadows Crew!

{Paul's wondering what's going on with the crew. So he calls Kym to find out what's going on.}

{Kym} Hello Paul.

{Paul} Kym! What's happening down there?

{Kym} We had a discussion with WS Markus.

{Paul} What did you guys talked about? Any last words of the communication process!?!

{Kym} Well Paul, Boom was the last word stated! Now we have to go talk to the rest of them.

{Paul} Ok, make them the offer. So we can work something out!

{Kym} You got it Paul!

THE BUTCHER IS BACK!

{Shawn and Brandon arrives at the airport, just in time for some lethal activities!}

{Shawn} I'm a call Kym, and let her know you here!

{Brandon} No! Better yet, call her and find out where they at! Don't alert them of my presence. Let be a surprise!

{Shawn} Hey! No problem, I got you partner! Calling her now. Hey Kym this Shawn, where you guys at?

{Kym} We're at the warehouse. You know, we going to be here till tomorrow. We have some unfinished business to tend to!

{Shawn} Cool! I just wanted to know y'all whereabouts. So I contact you on a moments notice.

{Brandon} So where are they?

{Shawn} At the new warehouse. You want me to get you there by limo!?!

{Brandon} No! Cab will be fine. Like I said, Surprise!

{Shawn calls a cab for Brandon to meet the crew at the warehouse, but Detectives Holman and Shultz are in search of Paul Meadows.}

{DT Holman} I wonder where Paul disappeared to?

{DT Shultz} Well he can do many tricks, and make like Houdini is one of them; as well as others!

{DT Holman} Yeah I bet! Including Mr. Daniels. That's why we can't find a trace of him. And now that case went cold!

{DT Shultz} I'm willing to bet that Paul has one more magic trick up his sleeve. Before he hauls ass out of town!

{DT Holman} Well damn Shultz . . . It seems like you know more about Paul and his crew than I do!?! So what make you think he's going to make a run for it! When you clearly stated that he runs from nothing or no one?

{DT Shultz} It's sheer mathematical, now think Holman. Do you truly believe that Paul is going to hang around too much longer!?! I don't think so!

{DT Holman} So what you think his last trick is going to be?

{DT Shultz} I don't know? But something tells me it's going to be truly; astronomically gangster; beyond compare.

{DT Holman} Well we better catch up with him before he hauls ass out of town. In which I doubt very seriously Paul Meadows will make a run for it. He'll fight first! Either way, let's go!

{So now the Meadows crew are on their way to the west side of town.}

{Kym} I wonder why Shawn wanted to know our whereabouts? It's not like he was concerned before, so why all of a sudden he wants to know!?! Seems pretty strange to me.

{Lavis} Aww Kym, don't be so suspicious! You know Shawn means well.

{Kym} Maybe your right. I'm just on my guard right now. All the shit we been going through lately!?!

{Rachel} Well in this life we're living, you got to suspect some shit to come back, hell even Paul himself! Got to know the boomerang effect!

{Paul} Montego we just about covered everything we needed to cover in New York. I'm gonna call Richard, and have him to help me with my grand finale.

{Montego} Really! What's that?

{Paul} You'll see! Believe me Montego, It's to die for!

{Montego} Wow! I hope I'm not on the death list!?!

{Paul} Nope!

{Paul calls Richard for him to help on the grand finale.}

{Richard} Hey what's good Paul?

{Paul} Richard my man! I'm going to need you to help me on something I call, The Grand Finale!

{Richard} Alright Paul! What you need?

{Paul explains to Richard some of the details to him. About the Grand Finale. But the crew is on the move to meet The Westsiders on their turf.}

{Rachel} You know Kym, this is really risky! We don't know what we may run into. I hope everyone is strapped.

{The crew replies, We are! But they're unaware that they are being followed.}

OUR EXISTENCE, COULD MEAN YOUR EXTINCTION!

{As the crew arrives at their hideout on the west part of town, they all exists out of the vehicle.}

{Kym} Alright you guys, y'all ready to take'em by storm!?!

{The Meadows Crew busts in on the Westsiders! Guns drawn! The Westsiders draws also!}

{Kym} Alright faggots! Put your weapons down, and we won't lay your asses down!

{WS Sweetpea} I don't know who you guys are!?! But I know you all better get the Hell out of here! While you still can!

{Lavis} Bitch! We didn't give you permission to talk! So, shut the hell up!

{WS Sweetpea} And who are you guys anyway!?!

{Kym} Allow me to introduce us, we are The Meadows Crew. You see we're here to give a fair warning. The police had been notified that you all were the ones that ran down on us. At our warehouse on the north end of town, and we were going to just light your asses up, but Paul sent us to let you know that; your man Markus! Dropped dime on all of you. So we have a proposition for you all.

{WS Sweetpea} Forget that bullshit! Westsiders Light'em up!

{The war was on! Lavis shot one down! Sweetpea bust off shots! Kym shoots one more down! Rachel firing off her twin glocks! At this time, through all the warfare. Brandon is creeping in the back way. Samantha sneaks up behind one of them. Grabs around the throat, puts her nine to the temple and shoot the guy brains out! Two of the Westsiders are heading out the back hallway, but Brandon's flying blades meets their foreheads!

{Brandon} Damn! Y'all didn't make it.

{Kym} Ok Sweetpea! You give up now, or what!?! You guys have no win with us! We're military trained! That's like putting a spoiled ass! Know it all three year old in the 12th grade. And pray they'll graduate!

{George} Yeah, put milk in mud and hope it makes cake! Nope, It ain't happening captain!

{Kym calls Paul to let him know their with the Westsiders.}

{Paul} Kym! You guys are all together huh!?!

{Kym} Yeah Paul, all in together now! So what you want us to do?

{Paul} It's time for them to take an all expense paid trip. Take them to the airport! Their tickets will be paid by the time you guys get there.

{Kym} Got Damn! Paul is so freaking generous!

{George} Well what did he say!?!

{Kym} Look! Westside remainers. Paul has so generously paid for the remaining balance of your crew, tickets to go to the Bahamas.

{Meadows Crew is looking in shock!}

{Lavis} What the Hell! Paul, why he sent us here for!?! To freaking give them a joyride after the spanking!?! It makes no sense!

{Samantha} Damn sure don't! So now what?

{Kym} We got to follow his orders. I don't understand it neither, but let's get them there.

{WS Sweetpea} Wait a minute! You mean to tell me, that Paul Meadows is paying for a ticket a piece for us? Something don't set right with me about the whole thang! What's the catch?

{Kym} No catch, just get to the airport! Before he changes his mind.

{So the crews leave for the airport. But Paul has other urgendas on his mind!}

{Paul} Montego! Part 1 of the grand finale is underway.

{Montego} Well what's going on!

{Paul} You'll know when it happens. Besides Richard's going to be there. He know what to do. Next, The Southsiderz in Baltimore! For them cats . . . Let me see. Oh yeah! Where's your boy!?!

{Montego} He's somewhere around! You want me to contact him?

{Paul} Yes! Tell him their location in Baltimore, MD. And then, it's time for a good old fashion barbeque.

{Montego} I know what that means, cook'em!

{Paul} I mean, Well Done!

CHAPTER 20

THE CROSSOVER

PAUL'S SINISTER SET UP.

{As the crew arrives at the airport with the Westsiders. Richard meets them at the gate 7 with tickets in his hands.}

{Richard} Welcome Westsiders! I have you're tickets out of dodge. I strongly advise, that you guys take the flight before things get out of hand.

{WS Sweetpea} Alright! We'll take the trip. We could use the vacay getaway, but don't think for one solitary moment that were finished. Just because we're taking a temporary peace offering.

{Richard} Oh I can assure you, that it's very temporary! But for now, let's just enjoy the getaway.

{WS Sweetpea} Word! Thanks, we're out! We will continue this conversation when we return.

{Richard} Kym, I'm a tell you this . . . This may not be they're first flight, but it will be they're last!

{Kym} What do you mean Richard!?!

{Richard} You'll see! Just wait till the plane gets of the ground! Oh it's in route for take off!

{The plane is going down the runway at the normal speed, but the landing gear is having technical difficulties of raising up. But little did the crew knew. That the plane was set for auto pilot, with a little surprise onboard.}

{WS Kenny} Hey Sweetpea, how come we're the only ones on this flight!?!

{WS Sweetpea} What you mean, we're the only ones onboard? Something's wrong with this picture.

{WS Larry} Yo! There's no pilot neither!

{WS Sweetpea} So who's flying the damn plane!?! This mofolo is on auto pilot!?!

{WS Kenny} This shit is a set up Sweetpea!

WALKING THE INVISIBLE LINE

{As the plane flying higher and higher, the altitude meter is aligned to the detonator switch that's linked to the C4 explosives in the cargo department of the plane.}

{Lavis} Richard what's going on with Paul? How come he wanted us to go spank the Westsiders, but then send them on a trip!

{Richard} We'll Crew . . . Take a look up in the friendly skies, and say bye bye!

{The crew looks up in confusion, but then the shock came about when the plane exploded in mid-flight.}

{Richard} Now does that answers y'all question about what Paul is doing? Huh I believe so! Now I can rest easy at night, and my wife can rest in peace. Oh yeah, Bye Bye Westside Wanksters!

{Kym} Got Damn Paul! We didn't expect that!

{Richard} Oh just wait girl! The best is yet to come.

{Samantha} Ok, I see you Paul! But we're hot now! If we weren't before. So you know Detectives Holman and his fellow officers will be on our trails. Harder than ever before!

{Richard} Don't worry about them right now! We got bigger fish to fry! As a matter of fact, we have to settle a score in Baltimore! Once and for all!

{Paul calls Kym and asks her about the show.}

{Kym} Hello!?! Oh Paul, it's you!

{Paul} Well Ms. Kym Lei, How you enjoyed the fireworks display. Enlightening wasn't it?

{Kym} Hell yeah! Very enlightening! Now what's going on for Baltimore?

{Paul} Not over the phone! I'll send instructions by Richard. Oh yeah . . . Tell Rich, Job well done!

{Kym} Hey Rich! Paul said, "Job well done!"

The Smell of Foul Play!

{The news didn't waste time getting out what happened to plane exploding in mid-flight! So now Detectives Holman and Shultz are on the case.}

{DT Holman} Wow! Plane explosion, what in the world is going on?

{Captain Harris} Alright Holman! I need you and your crew to find out what happened to that plane. So get moving Holman!

{DT Holman} No problem Captain! As usual..

{DT Shultz} What's up Holman?

{DT Holman} Well we are assigned to the case of the Exploding Plane that the news just casted, and the Captain just personally came to me. Recruiting us to this case!

{DT Shultz} What in GOD's Name!?!

{DT Holman} Yeap, let's go!

{Meanwhile Paul is on a heatwave of paybacks. No time to waste! He checks with Elm to see if he's in place in Baltimore.}

{Paul} Now Richard done handled part 1; of the grand finale Montego. So now, I'm going to check on Elm. Make sure he's on point.

{Montego} Don't worry Paul! I got Elm on point, he's always on time.

{Montego calls Elm.}

{Elm} What's going on Montego?

{Montego} Paul wants to make sure that you handle that business in Baltimore.

{Elm} Let Paul know . . . I got this! All he got to do, Is stay tuned! Until the next episode.

{Richard} How's that for a grade A disappearing act!?!

{Lavis} Wow! Now you see them, Now you don't!

{Kym} And Paul's no way's near finished.

{Richard} Nope!

{The Detectives arrives at the airport from where the plane took off. In hopes to find clues.}

{Officer Peele} Man that was a hell of a explosion!

{Officer Williams} Humph! Never mind Katie Kaboom huh!?!

{DT Holman} Ok enough of the wise cracks! Do we know how many casualties were onboard!?!

{DT Shultz} I believe it was about 10 of them, and according to the aviation official. Two groups was present before the plane took off. It was unclear about a pilot being onboard.

{DT Holman} Are you saying that the plane was on auto pilot at the time of take off!?!

{DT Shultz} Yeah that's what i'm saying. But nothing for certain yet!

{DT Holman} Ok! Guys I want every inch of the area searched thoroughly! No stones unturned, and search the aircraft asap! I want to check the video recordings on the grounds. To see who was present at the time of take off, and detonation of the explosion! Let's go! No time to waste.

{Elm is on his way to Baltimore, and Paul is waiting and anticipating the call from him. Stating that the job is done!}

{Richard} Look y'all I'm getting ready to head home. I have to get some sleep. George you need to do the same. Part 2 of Paul's Grand Finale is underway right now as we speak.

{George} Rich! What's next with Paul? Hell the plane bomb was breathtaking alone!

{Richard} Huh! That was nothing! Compared to what's up coming.

THERE'S NO FURY HOTTER THAN HELL

{Brandon} What's going on crew?

{Kym} You missed the battle and the fireworks of the Westsiders.

{Brandon} No I didn't. I was there when you all was in battle with those Westsiders. As a matter of fact, I took two of them out.

{Rachel} What; when!?!

{Brandon} Well it was kinda easy when they ran straight into me at the back of the warehouse. As I was coming in you guys were taking some of them out with y'all. So I followed you guys to the airport. I told Paul some time ago, you never know when I'll pop up!

{Richard} Well, make no mistake cause Paul is consolidating some troublesome assholes that's gotten on his last nerves!

{Kym} I know one in particular that's been given all of us a got damn headache! That damn Holman and Shultz and their merry men! Like he's Robin Hood and the Merry Faggots!

{The crew laughs.}

{Richard} Well I'll see you guys tomorrow! But don't be surprised to hear something tragic in the morning.

{Lavis} Like what Rich!?!

{Samantha} Yeah like what!?!

{Richard} We'll see won't we!

{Elm arrives in Baltimore, with destruction in his eyes, and malice in his heart. So he calls Paul with the updates.}

{Elm} Hello Paul, I'm in Ball MD. So where's the spot.

{Paul} On the side of town, where the snakes throwdown! S side baby; on the S side baby!

{Elm} I got you man! Get some sleep, and in the morning; check the news!

{Paul} Well, on that note. Goodnight!

{Elm says nothing more, he just hangs up.}

{Paul} Now that's service without a smile. Damn! Well goodbye Southsiderz!

{Elm arrives at the Southsiderz hideout, and lays down C4 around the building. As he was wiring up the C4. He was spotted by one of the Southsiderz.

{SS Wes} Yo! Who the Hell are you? And what are you doing!?!

{Elm wastes no time, pulls out his gun with silencer; and he shoots Wes dead in the head. Then pulls his lifeless body over the C4 canister. Lines up the wiring to the switch, and runs to the car. Closes the door and hits the switch. Kaboom!}

{Elm} Goodnight y'all, sleep tight!

{DT Holman} Well Shultz, what did you guys find out! Cause you know Captain Harris will be on my back unless we have something concrete to go by. He don't want to hear any excuses.

{DT Shultz} We found out the Meadows Crew was there before the plane took off. But we not sure if they're affiliated with the explosion.

{Officer Williams} Hey Holman! This just in, on the plane was 10 casualties. Oh and get this, they were rivals against the Meadows Crew.

{DT Holman} Keep talking!

{Officer Williams} They were from Florida, Miami to be exact! Coincidence . . . I think not!

{DT Holman} So, now what it looks like is. A plan of destruction to the Westsiders of Miami!

{Officer Williams} Correct Sir!

{DT Holman} Alright Shultz! It looks like we're going to have a discussion with the one, the only; Paul Meadows!

{DT Shultz} Ok, I gotta make a call. I'll be right with you!

THE DIABOLICAL PLOT

{As the Detectives were on they're way to catch up with Paul, They get the news about the bombing in Baltimore, MD.}

{DT Shultz} Now what about this Holman? You think Paul had something to do with this too?

{DT Holman} I wouldn't be surprised at all. With the mass connections he has, anythings possible for Paul Meadows and his Crew! Hell it's time to roll up on that ass! Before they cause any more damage, or casualties of war!

{The next morning Paul's waking up to the news.}

{Goodmorning Nashville! It's beautiful day out today. I'm Katie Washington bringing you this morning headline news from All Across America! An explosion at a abandon building on the Southside of Baltimore, Maryland. Has been reported that a group of young individuals, in which it was believed that a local gang was staying inside for a local hideout! Authorities stated that some 12 casualties were on the inside of the building, and one was on the outside of the building. Being that the body of the individual was severed. But the case is still under investigation, and we'll have more as the story unfolds!}

{Paul gets a call from Elm.}

{Elm} Goodmorning Paul, lovely day today isn't it?

{Paul} All I can say is, Well done! My Good, and Faithful Servant.

{Elm} Need me! You know how to find me.

{Paul} I do believe I will be needing you, one more time!

{Elm} Just have my pay ready, and it's a done deal! Oh by the way! Great barbeque yesterday. I really enjoyed the cookout, and those ribs were banging! Well I'll call you about the money you owe me for the food that we cooked.

{Paul} I got you Elm, and then some!

{Elm} I like that alot!

{Richard gets in contact with the crew early in the morning.}

{Kym} Goodmorning Richard, How are you?

{Richard} I'm good! Did you get a chance to see the news?

{Kym} No I didn't, what happened?

{Richard} Oh I advise you to tune in to the news, it can be very informative! Like right now.

{Kym turns to the news, and sees the tragedy that happened in Baltimore.}

{Kym} Well damn! Rest in peace y'all! Richard! What the hell Paul . . .

{Richard} Hush Kym! We got to get with the crew. So get off the phone so we can tell them to meet up at the warehouse. Pronto!

{Kym} You got it!

{Detectives are in route for Paul's office.}

{DT Holman} We going to get that damn Paul!

{DT Shultz} Man, you better open eyes Holman! Cause he's becoming Mr. Untouchable!

{DT Holman} Damn Shultz! Who side are you on man!?! Cause you been more on favor of not catching Paul Meadows and his Crew! So what's up?

{DT Shultz} Ok! Ok! Look we're here now. Let's go and get him!

{Paul and Montego in the warehouse awaiting for the crew to show up.}

{Richard calls Kym to see if she contacted the others.}

{Richard} Hey Kym, did you contact the others?

{Kym} Yes! They should be at the warehouse in a few minutes.

{Richard} Good! I'll be there momentarily myself. Paul and Montego should be there already. He said that it's about time for the grand finale.

{Meanwhile Holman; Shultz, and the other officers are closing in on the warehouse.}

{Paul} Montego, my crew should be arriving shortly. Ah, here they come now, little by little! Hi Rachel; George; Brandon; Lavis; Samantha. Now waiting for Richard and Kym. I was hoping that Porshia were coming as well.

{Rachel} She's still weak right now, but I always keep her updated with the new developments.

{Paul} I got something in store, to show my pain in the ass followers. First I need to call my informant.

A Switch for the Grand Finale!

{Paul calls his informant, and finds out that they're in position to reveal the information before The Grand Finale!}

{Richard and Kym arrives at the same time.}

{Richard} Kym, I wanted to see the look on your face after you saw the news this morning!

{Kym} Well look into my eyes, and you can see a portion of disbelief I had this morning. Paul ain't nothing to mess with!

{Richard} Girl, you should've remembered that from the war back in Afghanistan!

{Kym} Yeah, you're right! He was worst back then.

{Paul} Well well! Here's my other two of the crew! Just only missing one! Well Meadows crew, the reason I called for you guys this morning is to let you know. Soon I'll be going away for a while, and I'm nominating Richard and Montego. To run my business while I'm gone. Kym you're still in charge for ladies, but your responsibilities has increased. PG's are the same. Lavis; George; and Brandon, handle the guns. Along with the PG's as well. Samantha you're with Kym. As the crew in a nutshell, do what you gotta do. I expect nothing less, but the best! Is that clear Meadows Crew!

{They all replied, Yes Sir!}

{Just then, The Detectives came in the warehouse, on a mission to take down Paul!}

{DT Holman} Alright Paul Meadows! Your time is up! Come with me.

{Paul} What!?! You know what Holman, I got a surprise for you, and everybody else. There has been an informant amongst y'all! Now it's time to reveal! Informant Step forth!

{Everybody is in shock to find out the informant!}

{DT Shultz} That's right! It's me Holman! I've been on Paul's payroll ever since. Every move you made, every step you took; Paul's been watching you Through me fool! I've been telling all the long! Ever since you started going after Paul, I warned you! But you didn't listen to me. I told you, Paul is not the one you go after, unless you knew what you were doing. And you didn't! So now what!?!

{DT Holman} You mother freaking traitor! Benedict Arnold mofolo!

{DT Shultz} Yeah yeah! I know, but I told you. There were leaks in the department, didn't I!?!

{The two started tussling, and Paul instructed his crew to leave since they're not in question. But to go across the street and watch how I end all of the calamity.

{Richard} I don't know what you got up your sleeve Paul, but these two Detectives is going to tear down our warehouse.

{Paul} That's why two days ago I had Jason to move all the supplies to another location. 561 Trade Street in Chattanooga. All waiting for you guys. So go, and start handling the business tomorrow. You guys know your positions! Now handle it. I'll tend to these guys, now go! All of you go now!

{The crew leaves out the warehouse, and goes across the street. The officers arrives afterwards.}

{Paul calls Elm, to see if he took care of the last part of the finale.}

{Paul} Did you do that Elm?

{Elm} Are you there at the warehouse!?!

{Paul} Yes! Do it now!

{Richard} I wonder what's taking Paul so long, It's just him and the two detectives in there still fighting!

{Just then as they turned and looked, the warehouse exploded!}

{Kym} Oh My GOD! Noooo!

{Richard} What the Hell! No Paul! Noooo!

{The crew was staring in shock, and most couldn't even move. In disbelief that Paul didn't make it out of there in time! The police are also in disbelief as well.}

{Rachel} Nooo! Help them out of there! I don't give a damn! Help them!

The Conclusion

Wow! Paul Meadows really asked for more than what he was bargaining for huh!?! It's been a long travel since they were in the war. We are in hope that the crew can survive without their leader. So now it's on for the Meadows Crew to carry on for Paul. But what a switch, that Detective Shultz was an informant for Paul! Damn, we didn't see that one coming. Well warning comes before destruction, and Holman can't say that he wasn't warned. I guess that's what happens when you think you know everything; and you don't know nothing! At least not enough to go after a notorious mob figure. A gangster in a suit, huh watch you step officers. Cause remember, now Richard and Montego are in charge. So now what the law is going to do? Only "Walking the Invisible Line" part 2 can tell. But until then, hang on in there! Gangster Lovers! Oh, by the way . . . That's how you go out; with a BANG!

Written & Created By:
Alton R. House

www.ingramcontent.com/pod-product-compliance
Lightning Source LLC
Chambersburg PA
CBHW070938190726
48292CB00004B/1227